ESCAPE TO INISHBEG COVE

IZZY BAYLISS

Copyright © 2022 by Izzy Bayliss

All rights reserved.

No part of this book may be reproduced in any form or by any electronic or mechanical means, including information storage and retrieval systems, without written permission from the author, except for the use of brief quotations in a book review.

This novel is entirely a work of fiction. The names, characters, and incidents portrayed in it are the work of the author's imagination. Any resemblance to actual persons, living or deceased, events or localities is purely coincidental.

For Lila.

Love you, darling girl.

1

The November sunlight glistened white on the tears that fell down Grace O'Neill's pale face, and the sickly smell of freshly dug earth was cloying in her nostrils. The curled petals of a bouquet of red roses stood out jarringly against the glistening clay. The long line of mourners who had queued up to express their condolences had finally petered out, so it was just Grace and her aunt Maggie left standing at the graveside. Even though her mother had left Inishbeg Cove many years ago, Grace was touched by how many people had turned out to pay their respects. As the mourners gripped her hand tightly and whispered words of comfort, she had tried her best to keep the tears at bay.

'I can't believe that's it.' Grace turned to her aunt, her bottom lip quivering. 'I-I can't believe I'll never see Mum again.'

Maggie reached across and squeezed her niece's hand tightly with her own. 'I know, love.'

Grace saw tears burning in her aunt's eyes as she shook her head in disbelief.

'It just doesn't feel real, does it?'

'I already miss her so much. I know at thirty-one years of age I'm a fully grown woman, but I still don't feel ready for the world without my mother in it.'

'Look, I was thinking, Gracie...' Maggie began. 'You don't need to rush back to Dublin, do you? Why don't you stay on with me in Inishbeg Cove for a few days?' She put an arm around her niece's shoulder.

Grace wiped fresh tears away with the back of her hand and used a balled-up tissue to dab at her dripping nose. 'Maybe I will, Maggie. I don't think I could face the house in Dublin right now without Mum there.'

'There's no point in both of us being alone at a time like this,' Maggie said, patting her own eyes with a tissue. 'I'd be glad of the company, to be honest.'

Grace took a last look back at the cold earth where her mother now lived, feeling her breath snag in her chest. How was it possible that her mother was no longer with them? The woman who had been so full of life, who sang out of tune with the radio, the woman who buttered scones too thickly with butter, even though her doctor had warned her that her cholesterol was too high. The woman who could never throw anything out, and was usually 'upcycling' some tatty piece of old furniture that she had found hidden down the back of a charity shop. The woman who always ended her phone calls with 'I love you, Gracie'. The woman with an indomitable spirit. How was she gone?

Even though Grace and her mother had lived in Dublin, it had been her mother Rosa's dying wish that she be buried in Inishbeg Cove, which was the village where she had been born. Rosa had been a secondary school art teacher. Every summer since Grace had been born, they had left the traffic and busy streets of Dublin behind them and come to stay with Maggie in her coastguard cottage. Grace had loved it when Rosa and Maggie got together, and the three of them became their own family unit for the summer. Grace had never known her father so, after her mother, Maggie had been the closest adult to Grace growing up. She had adored her aunt. Like Rosa, Maggie had never married; Grace knew that Maggie had been engaged once before, but she never spoke about it. When the three O'Neill girls got together every summer, they were as thick as thieves. They would spend the long days of summer down in the cove, Grace running across the honeycomb sand, the salty air breezing over her skin, while Rosa and Maggie watched on. After dinner, her mother and aunt would open a bottle of wine while Grace had hot chocolate, and they would stay up late into the night, giggling. They were her happiest childhood memories.

As they made their way out of the cemetery, leaves in shades of mustard and rust rained down. They pushed the little gate closed behind them and emerged into St Brigid's churchyard, which was bathed in white wintry sunlight.

'Come on, love,' Maggie said, putting an arm around Grace's shoulder as if reading her thoughts. 'She'll always live on in here.' She thumped a fist against her heart.

They began to walk back through the village and along the coast road that led towards Maggie's cottage, the house where the O'Neill sisters had grown up. As the road climbed higher, Grace looked out over the green-grey water in the cove. Gulls squawked above them, searching for sea creatures left behind by the outgoing tide. How different the sea looked at this time of year, she thought. The bright cerulean blue shades of summer seemed a distant memory now.

When they reached Maggie's cottage they went inside. The cottage was small, with just two bedrooms, a bathroom and an open-plan kitchen and living area. Grace looked around the kitchen, which was in disarray as usual. The wooden counter tops were cluttered and a dresser stuffed with odds and ends ran along the back wall. A circular table and four chairs stood in the middle of the room and a small two-seater sofa and an armchair faced the large open fireplace, which still had the black iron hooks from the days when food was cooked in pots suspended over the turf. An easel stood in the corner, holding a canvas that Maggie was working on. Maggie was a painter: she usually painted seascapes and local scenes from around the cove, and as a result sold most of her work to tourists. To the side of the easel, old newspapers were piled up. Grace had offered to recycle them for her aunt numerous times, but she liked to keep them 'just in case', so the pile seemed to climb higher every time Grace came to visit. Maggie had a use for everything and hated throwing stuff out. It had always been a running joke between the three of them that Maggie wasn't a big fan of housework. Grace's stomach lurched at the reminder of her mother and the good-natured fun they used to have, teasing Maggie about her messy home.

'I'll light the fire if you want to go and freshen up, then we'll have a cup of tea,' Maggie said, rubbing her hands together to warm them.

Grace stood at the door of her mother's bedroom and took a deep breath. Even after Rosa had moved to Dublin at the age of seventeen, leaving Maggie to live alone in their childhood home, Maggie had kept her younger sister's bedroom for her, referring to it as 'Rosa's room'. Grace's maternal grandparents had died before she was born; as a result, the sisters had been fiercely close. Grace pushed open the door. As she entered the bedroom, her mother's scent still lingered on the air. Instantly tears filled her eyes and clogged her throat until it was hard to breathe. She looked around the simple white bedroom. The small case that Grace had brought with her when she had arrived the day before for the funeral stood unpacked in the corner. A blue-striped rug lay on the varnished floorboards and white bedlinen clothed the steel-framed bed. She and her mother had shared this bed whenever they had come to visit Maggie. The two of them would curl up beside one another, slotting together like spoons, listening to the soothing lullaby of the waves rolling in and out of the cove. It had been one of Grace's favourite things about their time in the village. Suddenly the room felt impossibly big and empty without her mother.

She walked over and opened the pine wardrobe where Rosa's colourful clothing still hung, as if waiting for her to come back. Her mother had kept a set of clothes here – mainly summer clothes but there were also some warmer jumpers and a bright yellow rain jacket. Her mother had always dressed extrovertly in brightly coloured prints and patterns – the bigger the clash, the better, as far as Rosa was concerned. Grace lifted out a turquoise oversized sweater that had been one of her mother's favourites. Rosa had proudly told her daughter that it was older than Grace was – she had even worn the baggy jumper throughout her pregnancy. If Grace closed her eyes, she could still see her mother in the jumper with her thumbs poking out through the holes that were ripped in the sleeves.

She lifted out the jumper and held it up to her face, rubbing the soft cashmere against her skin and breathing in the scent of her mother. It was a soothing mixture of her perfume and the washing powder she always used.

She put the sweater back into the wardrobe, went into the small bathroom next door and splashed water on her face. Then she returned to the living area, where the hearth glowed orange with the beginnings of a fire that Maggie had just lit.

'How are you doing, lovey?' Maggie asked her niece softly as she placed a pot of tea on the coffee table.

Grace flopped down onto the lumpy, misshapen sofa. 'Everywhere I turn there are reminders of her. I keep picking up my phone to call her and tell her how awful I'm feeling, but then I remember that I can't.'

'We'll get each other through it. I feel the same way,' Maggie said, sitting down beside her. 'I won't lie; it's going to be painful for the next while. The wound is going to sting and sting, but I remember after your grandparents died that gradually the pain dulls a little – it's like it moves down from the surface and gets deeply embedded into your heart. It'll still be there, but it won't take your breath away every time you remember.'

'I feel so lost. I have no one now – Mum is dead and I have no siblings. I feel like my anchor to the world is gone.' In the aftermath of losing her mother, Grace had realised with stark clarity that her connection to family was tenuous now, as if she was hanging onto the world by a thread. Maggie was the only relative she had left. Grace had never met her father; Rosa had raised her single-handedly and had always shut down every attempt Grace had made to find out who he was. Then when her mother had got sick, Grace hadn't wanted to distress her by bringing it up again. Although her mother had had no shortage of admirers over the years, Rosa had never opened her heart to another man, and so, Grace had been an only child. Growing up, Grace couldn't help but notice a lingering sadness in her mother's eyes whenever she had dared to raise the subject of her father; she had always wondered if her mother's heart had been too broken to allow another man into her life again.

'And what am I?' Maggie asked, pretending to be offended.

'Sorry, Maggie, I didn't mean it like that ... but I just feel ... well ... a bit lost right now.'

'I know what you meant, lovey, don't worry.' She placed a kindly hand over Grace's.

'Usually when you lose a parent, you have the other one, or you might have a brother or sister, but I only ever had Mum,' Grace went on. She couldn't help noticing Maggie's gaze dart to the floor at the mention of her father. Grace took a deep breath. 'Maggie?' She had wanted to ask this question so many times, but could never seem to find the right words.

'Uh-huh?'

'I was wondering if you knew who my father was,' she tried. He had never been in her life, and Grace knew that you couldn't miss somebody you had never known, yet she still found herself yearning for the connection that her friends had with their fathers. She would look at strange men in the street and wonder if they might be her father. She felt as though she was always searching for him. Although Grace had had a very loving and secure home, a part of her had craved a normal upbringing with a mother and father, maybe even a sibling or two as well. She felt awful admitting that to herself, and she could never have said that to her mother. If she just knew who her father was, Grace was sure she would feel less at sea; her life would have more anchors in it.

'Ah, Gracie, what are you bringing that up for again?'

'Please, Maggie. If you know who he is, won't you tell me?'

Maggie shifted uncomfortably. 'Look, don't be troubling yourself with all that. Your mother was both a mother and a father to you growing up. She did a great job raising you.'

Shame flooded Grace. Her mother was only just hours in the ground and now Maggie thought she was betraying her memory. She knew it hadn't been easy for her mother, raising her single-handedly.

'I know, Maggie. It's just sometimes, I wish I knew who he was…' she said wistfully. 'Did she ever tell you his name, even?' If she had something to go on, no matter how small the information, it would be a start.

Maggie shook her head. 'I'm sorry, love.'

Grace's heart fell. If Maggie didn't know, then there was no hope of Grace ever finding out. Her mother had taken her father's name to her grave with her and now Grace had to accept that she would probably never learn who he had been.

2

Strong morning sunlight cracked around the edge of the curtain as Grace opened her eyes the next morning. She had a blissful few seconds when she woke where she thought she was on holiday in Inishbeg Cove, her mother lying next to her in the bed. Grace had stretched out her arm across the cotton sheets to reach for her mother, but the bed was startlingly cool on that side, and then she had remembered the awfulness. The shock hit her with brutal force. Her mother was gone.

She climbed out of bed, dressed, then began to tidy the mess in kitchen. She started by clearing the counter tops, putting food away into the cupboards beneath and washing the dishes. It was as she was drying the crockery that she had a brainwave: perhaps her mother, although unable to tell Grace about her paternity when she was alive, had left details in her will for Grace to learn after her death. She was filled with fresh hope; maybe she had a chance of discovering who her father had been after all. She checked her watch and saw that it was still too early to call Barry Walsh, her mother's solicitor, who was based in Dublin. It would be at least another hour before the working world opened.

As soon as her watch read nine, she picked up her phone and dialled the number. Her call was answered by a breathless receptionist; Grace guessed she had sprinted to her desk to get to the call. She introduced herself as Rosa O'Neill's daughter, and was eventually put through to Barry Walsh. She had met him on a couple of occasions when she had gone with her mother to see him after she had been given the devastating news that her breast cancer was terminal and she needed to put her affairs in order.

'Ah yes, I am so sorry to hear about your mother. Look, Grace, we don't normally do this over the phone, but seeing as you're the executor and you were present when her will was drafted...' he began. She heard him rifle through papers in the background. Eventually he began to read out the will. He confirmed what she already knew: that her mother was leaving her estate to her, including their house in Ranelagh. He fell silent when he had finished reading and Grace held her breath, wondering if there might be something more that he was going to add.

'Is that it?' Grace asked as the silence stretched between them. 'Is there a letter or something else that she might have included for me?'

'I'm afraid that's all there is, Grace,' he said. 'Were you expecting something more?'

'No, sorry...'

Barry cleared his throat. 'Are you okay, Grace?'

'Yes, I'm fine, thank you.' Grace tried her best to keep the tang of disappointment from her voice. She was no closer to finding out the truth about her father.

'Who was that?' Maggie asked a few moments later as

she came into the kitchen, wearing a baggy nightshirt. Her wild curls stuck up chaotically from sleep.

'Mum's solicitor.'

Maggie took in Grace's tear-filled eyes. 'It's not bad news, is it, love?' she asked with concern.

'I stupidly thought she might have named my father in her will,' Grace blurted, feeling foolish.

'Oh, darling,' Maggie said, rushing over and putting an arm around her shoulder. 'Come on, why are you letting it bother you so much? You've got to the ripe old age of thirty-one without him in your life and you've managed perfectly fine.'

'I know, but I can't explain it. Since Mum died, I just have this ... this ... thing in my head about finding him. I want to know more about where I came from.'

'This is where you came from,' Maggie said, gesturing around the four walls of the tiny cottage. 'Your mum was born here, and your grandmother. This is where the O'Neill girls are from.'

Grace was instantly contrite. 'I'm sorry – you're right, Maggie.' She knew that there must have been a reason her mother hadn't wanted her to know who her father was, and she should respect that. It wasn't fair to her mother for her to go digging around in her past now that she was no longer with them. For all Grace knew, her father could have been a horrible person and she was better off without him in her life.

Maggie surveyed her living room. In it everything looked orderly for once: the cushions had been plumped and straightened, the pile of old newspapers was gone, and the dust that cloaked the clutter on the shelves seemed to have disappeared. 'Did you clean this place up?'

Grace nodded ruefully. 'I couldn't sleep, and cleaning helps to distract me.'

'Are you sure you're related to me?' Maggie laughed. They had always joked that Grace couldn't possibly be related to Maggie, such was her love of cleaning.

'I hope you don't mind?'

'Mind? Are you crazy? I have plenty more jobs for you to do if you feel like going on a cleaning spree.'

Despite the ache in her heart, Grace couldn't help crack a smile at her aunt.

'I was thinking we might head down to the cove for a swim after breakfast – what do you say?' Maggie said.

'In November! Are you mad?' Rosa and Maggie had been lifelong sea-swimmers and whenever her mother came home, the first thing she always did was head for a dip in the cove, no matter what the weather. It was her way of getting reacquainted with the village after her absence. Grace had often joined Rosa and Maggie for a sea-swim in the summer months, but never at this time of the year.

'Well, we swim all year round down here. C'mon, it's the best medicine for you right now.'

Grace knew that Maggie could be a bit evangelical about her love of sea-swimming; she reckoned she had seen people's lives transformed by the daily ritual of bathing in the salty water. Although Grace was sceptical about her aunt's claims, she didn't have the energy to protest.

'It'll clear your head, I promise,' Maggie continued. 'And I need to drop in some paintings to Ruairí in the café so I'll treat you to a slice of lemon drizzle cake afterwards. How does that sound?' Ruairí displayed Maggie's art on the café walls for his customers to purchase, as did the gift shop in the nearby town of Ballymcconnell.

'Well that seals the deal,' Grace said. Her aunt knew Ruairí's lemon drizzle cake was her weakness.

After a breakfast of sausages, rashers and eggs, which neither of them seemed to have the appetite for, Maggie and Grace put on their rain jackets and headed out into the drizzle. Grace had found an old swimsuit belonging to her mother in one of her drawers; even though it was several sizes too big and was covered with bright red poppy flowers, it would do the job.

As they descended the coast road towards the cove, the sea glistened silver and in the distance fishing boats were already returning with their catch. Below them, the village looked like a model, with matchstick people walking about and going into tiny shops. She breathed in deeply and noticed there was something different about the air here compared to back at home in Dublin: when she breathed it into her lungs, it felt cleansing and calmed her body and mind.

Maggie and Grace walked along the headland until they finally arrived at the dunes. They saw the swimmers gathered at their usual place by the rocks. They were laughing and joking easily with one another as they stripped off in the face of a keen north-westerly wind. Grace couldn't help wincing as they ran into the cool water. People of all ages: wrinkly, older bodies stood beside slender, toned young people and nobody batted an eyelid as they entered the water together. She followed Maggie over towards the swimmers, taking the path that cut through the dunes.

'Another recruit?' an older man, his skin loosened by age, asked as he unbuttoned his shirt beside her.

'This is my niece, Grace,' Maggie said. 'This is Frank.' She gestured to the man. 'And this is Laura and Imelda...' Maggie listed names until Grace's head was spinning, trying to remember them all. She recognised several of the faces from her mother's funeral the day before.

'We're so sorry for your loss,' they said in turn as Maggie introduced them. All Grace could do was nod in thanks as the loss of her mother pierced her heart once more.

She saw that Maggie had begun undressing, so she did the same. As she tentatively peeled down her leggings, the bitter wind clawed at her skin. She noticed that none of the other swimmers wore a wetsuit; they all seemed to be hardened to the elements. The only concession Maggie had made to the cold was to give Grace a pair of neoprene booties to stop her feet from going numb. She slipped them on her feet. It was one thing going sea-swimming in the summer months, but stripping down to her bare skin in November brought a new meaning to the word 'cold'.

She folded her clothes and stuffed them inside her backpack. Even with the shelter of the cove, it felt as though the wind would cut her in two, and she shivered on the sand as she followed Maggie towards the water.

The icy Atlantic rushed up along the sand to meet her toes and then, as she stepped forward some more, the cold waves swirled around her ankles, giving her a sharp shock. She looked across at Maggie, who was charging through the water like a woman possessed, already up to her thighs.

'Come on,' she called to Grace. 'It's easier if you just run straight in. Mind over matter.'

'I can't—' Grace called back to her. She kept walking until the water reached her ankles. The rippled sea bed sloped beneath her feet, making her feel unsteady. She kept going. Then the sand dropped away dramatically and the water was over her knees. Despite the booties, her feet were numb; she couldn't feel them move under her. This was madness. Why on earth was she doing this?

'Just throw yourself in! I promise you, my dear, it's the best way,' Maggie encouraged.

A large wave rushed in and splashed Grace's thighs, causing her to squeal with shock.

'At least you're in now.' Maggie laughed. 'Duck down and get your waist in and then lie back, like I'm doing.'

Grace did as she was told, feeling the chill of the water like a slap on her torso as she let it envelop her body. Slowly, she lifted one foot at a time off the sea floor, then tilted her body backwards and allowed the briny water to buoy her up. The water didn't seem as cold any more – in fact, it felt warmer beneath the blanket of the sea than above. As she floated in the petrol-blue ocean, staring up at the slate-grey sky above her, she suddenly got it. A feeling of great calm washed over her as the waves pushed in and bobbed her along. She was weightless. The water was so cold that her mind couldn't think about anything else. Her grief was temporarily suspended as she floated in the water. It was almost spiritual.

She looked across at Maggie and grinned. Maggie smiled back at her.

'I told you!' Maggie said.

When Grace got out of the water, the only word she could use to describe how she felt was 'euphoric'. She was on top of the world. She had swum in the freezing Atlantic Ocean in November! She had surrendered herself to it completely and had felt at one with the water. It had been exhilarating.

She shivered on the sand as she towelled off. Some of the group wore Dry Robes while others had brought dressing gowns, like her. As she wrapped its fleecy warmth around her, she was glad Maggie had suggested she bring it.

'Would you like a biscuit?' Maggie offered after they had

all dressed. She passed around a packet of ginger nuts. Grace used her thumbs to push one out before passing the packet along.

Then Maggie handed her a mug of coffee poured from her thermos flask. As Grace curled her hands around the steaming mug, savouring its warmth, she felt fortified. Like taking paracetamol for a headache, swimming in the sea had been a temporary pain relief for her grieving heart.

3

The smell of thyme and tarragon greeted Penny Murphy before she had even set foot inside the house, and she guessed that Tadgh was cooking again. She let herself in and closed the door behind her, shutting out the bitter Atlantic wind. She went into the kitchen and saw him standing at the hob.

'Hi, love,' she said, lifting the strap of her cross-body bag over her head and putting the bag down on the table.

'There you are!' He put down the spoon he had been using to stir the pot, came over and wrapped his strong arms around her. 'How was your day?'

'Good – we had a busy morning.' Penny was still working alongside Ruairí in the café in the mornings while Lucy was at playschool. Although she had initially been hired to help Ruairí during the busier summer months, the two of them worked well together and so she had become a permanent fixture in the café. 'The swimmers were all in. What are you cooking now?' She surveyed the Shaker-style kitchen in the house that had recently become her home. Pots and pans of various sizes lay piled up around the sink.

'There are no kitchen porters here,' she admonished good-naturedly.

'I thought I'd make us a chicken pie for dinner. Lucy will eat that, won't she?'

'Lucy would eat anything you make. It smells delicious.' She reached up and traced her finger down over the jagged scar in his eyebrow that was the only tell-tale sign of his brush with death just two months earlier. It was still quite pink and raised, but she knew it would fade in time. Penny felt a surge of gratitude every time she looked at him. She couldn't believe that they had been given a second chance. To think that this time last year she had still been unhappily married to her artist husband, Joe de Paor: his mood swings, long silences and withdrawn behaviour, had made her question everything she did, leaving her to wonder what she had done wrong or what she might have said to upset him. It hadn't been until she and Lucy had left him in Dublin and returned to Inishbeg Cove, the tiny coastal village where she had been born, that she had realised just how much they were suffering living with him and his unpredictable temper. At first she had been broken-hearted when Joe told her that he needed space from her, but leaving Dublin to return to her childhood home had been the best thing she had done for herself and her daughter. Then of course she had bumped into Tadgh, her first love, and realised that the spark between them had never quite gone out. They had broken up following the death of his parents in a tragic road traffic accident when Tadgh had been just eighteen. As Tadgh had struggled through his grief, he had taken over his parents' restaurant while caring for his younger brother Senan, who had been only six at the time. The weight of responsibility that had been thrown upon Tadgh at such a young age meant that Penny and Tadgh had had to deal with feelings that were bigger than the both of them, and far beyond their tender teenage years and so eventually, they had gone their separate ways. Penny had moved to Dublin for university shortly afterwards and they hadn't set eyes on one another again until she had met him in the cove not long after she had returned to the village. Although she hadn't wanted to admit it initially, she had quickly realised that the flame had never gone out between them. Finally everything had fallen into place and she knew her heart belonged to Tadgh. She had just worked up the courage to tell Joe that their marriage was over, when Tadgh was hit by a falling tree as the village was battered by a wild Atlantic storm. As she sat by his bed in hospital, willing him to pull through, she had sworn that, if he survived, she would never let him out of her life again. She had lost him once as a teenager, she had nearly lost him a second time in the storm, and she wasn't going to let it happen a third time. Now, not a day went by when she didn't pinch herself. She was so lucky – it was finally their time at last. This was her chance at happiness, and she was grabbing it with both hands.

She and Lucy had recently moved in with Tadgh. They had been spending all their time together anyway, and it felt like the natural next step for their relationship. Senan had left Inishbeg Cove in September to study hospitality at college. Penny's parents Rita and Pat were thrilled that she and Lucy were putting down roots in the village. They had adored Tadgh ever since they'd been together as teenagers. Her mother had never understood why Tadgh and Penny had broken up in the first place. Lucy had recently started at the local playschool, run by the very patient Josephine, and Rita and Pat collected her every day and brought her back to their house until Penny finished working in the café after the lunchtime rush. Lucy had already made lots of friends, and arrived home each day singing new songs and recounting tales about her day. As she ran around the cove, collecting shells left behind by the tide or poking sea creatures to see if they moved, Penny could see how much happier her daughter was. Lucy had arrived a shy, nervous child, but had recently come out of her shell and clearly loved village life. Although she was only three, it pained Penny to think how the strained atmosphere in their Dublin home might have affected her daughter without her even realising. Joe still hadn't come down to visit Lucy since he had stormed back to Dublin; she had offered to bring Lucy to Dublin to see him, but he had said he was too busy working on a commission. Penny dearly hoped, for her daughter's sake, that he would make an effort to be involved in her life.

The oven beeped. Tadgh hurried over and opened the door. 'I've made apple tart for dessert,' he called over his shoulder as he put on oven gloves then lifted the dish out.

'Although it's lovely to have a three-course dinner every day, I'm not sure my waistline agrees. If you keep feeding me at this rate, I'm going to be huge.' Her jeans had already grown tighter since she'd moved in with Tadgh. Her mother said she looked all the better for it; Penny knew she had been skin and bone when she had arrived in the village at the start of the summer. Her clothes had been hanging off her and her face had been gaunt and shadowed because stress had stolen her appetite. Now it was back with a bang because she was happy and if a few extra pounds were the price she had to pay, Penny could live with that. For the first time in years, she was at peace. Her heart was content.

'I guess that's one of the hazards of living with a chef.' He grinned with her. 'I like feeding people. I miss the restaurant so much.' As both the head chef and manager, Tadgh had had no choice but to close the restaurant while he recovered from his accident.

She surveyed the messy kitchen. 'I never would have guessed,' she said sardonically.

'Actually, I was thinking ... I might go back to work,' he tried.

Penny was shocked. 'But the doctors said it would be a few more weeks before you were fully recovered.'

'Well, it would just be for a few hours initially. My rehab is going really well. I think I've recovered faster than anyone expected. I checked with my physiotherapist and he said he'd be happy to allow me back once I promised to take it easy. I could go back slowly and build it back up from there.'

Penny came over, put her arms around his neck and looked at his handsome face. She knew its every angle and contour intimately. 'As much as I love having you cook for me, your kitchen is where you belong. If you feel ready and the physio thinks it's okay, then why not?'

His face lit up. 'Really?'

'Maybe we could even have a little party to mark the occasion,' Penny suggested. 'What do you think?'

'That's a great idea! Getting a second chance after the accident ... finally being with you ... they're things to celebrate. And it will be a nice way to tell customers that I'm back open. We can invite everyone,' he continued excitedly. 'A celebration for the whole village!'

'I said a *little* party. You're meant to be taking it easy!' she chided, but her heart swelled to see how animated he was becoming as the plans took off in his head. She knew how much he missed being in his restaurant.

4

One week later, Grace climbed the worn steps over the crumbling stone wall that led into the cemetery. She had finally plucked up the courage to visit her mother's grave. Grace hadn't been ready to face it since the awful day of the funeral, but guilt was getting the better of her. She wasn't sure if she believed in an afterlife but, if there was such a thing, she would hate for her mother to think that she had forgotten about her.

Grace was slowly starting to emerge from the haze of her grief. She was still staying with Maggie, because the thought of returning to the empty house in Dublin she had shared with her mother was overwhelming. She wasn't sure how long she would stay in Inishbeg Cove, but for now she needed to feel connected to her mother, and she felt that most strongly when she was in the village, cocooned from the reality of her world.

Maggie and Grace had fallen into an easy routine where they would rise and have breakfast together each day before going for a swim. Despite her initial reluctance, Grace was reaping the benefits of sea-swimming. Her skin had never been better. She usually had patches of eczema along her arms, but they had all cleared up, and when she looked in the mirror she noticed that her face had also taken on a better pallor over the last few days.

Her head was better for it too. Maggie had been right about sea-swimming helping to calm her mind; when she was in the water, her extremities feeling numb, she wasn't able to think about anything except how bloody cold it was. She didn't think about the grief that still ripped her in two every time she remembered that her mother was no longer with them. She didn't think about the guilt she carried because, no matter how often Maggie told her that she didn't need her father in her life, she still longed to know who he was. When she was in the water, she didn't have to think about what she was going to do with her future; when her mother had been diagnosed with terminal cancer, Grace had resigned from her job as an accountant to care for Rosa, and now Grace was questioning whether being an accountant was really what she wanted to do with her life after all. The creative genes ran strong through the O'Neill women and Grace had always been drawn to more artistic pursuits. She loved sketching and had a good eye for interiors too, but she lacked confidence in her talent, and so, rather than risk an artistic life like her mother and her aunt had done, she had sensibly chosen to study a degree in accountancy because of the secure job prospects it offered. 'You'll never see an out-of-work accountant', her career guidance teacher at school had advised her. Security was what Grace had craved her whole life, but if her mother's untimely death had taught her anything, it was that life was too short to do a job you hated.

As she floated in the cold water every morning, feeling the low sunlight warm her face, she could forget all her worries, and her head was at peace for a few minutes. There was something about connecting with the elements in their rawest form that helped her to plough through her grief.

Even though Grace was by far the youngest member of the group, the sea-swimmers had all welcomed her wholeheartedly and she looked forward to meeting them every day. They were men and women of all ages, shapes and sizes, and she loved the camaraderie they shared as they bathed together. They didn't all come every day; people worked different hours or had things on, but there were usually a few people gathered when Maggie and Grace arrived at eleven o'clock. After they emerged from the sea, some of them liked to pick seaweed from the shoreline and drape it around their shoulders for its skin-healing properties. Then the group would stand around drinking steaming tea or coffee from their flasks and passing around a packet of biscuits. They had a routine that Grace found strangely reassuring, at a time when it seemed as though the bottom had fallen out of her world.

Grace made her way deeper into the cemetery, which was shaded by ancient oak trees, passing older headstones covered in lichen and moss, bent forward by the weight of time. She headed towards the newer graves at the back, where her mother was buried. The silence was only pierced by the screeching and cawing of the gulls that arced above her. Soon she had arrived at the mound of fresh earth with a simple wooden cross marking the spot. She would need to organise a headstone at some stage, she knew, but it seemed overwhelming to think of Rosa's short life etched in cold marble. It was still difficult to accept that her beautiful mother lay beneath the soil and was never coming back.

She sat down on the edge of a nearby grave, looked around her to make sure she was alone, and then began talking to her mum. She told her how she still hadn't gone back to Dublin and had been staying with Maggie for the last week. She told her that they went swimming every day. As she began to talk, the words spilled from her lips and she forgot that she was in the cold cemetery. It felt like she was sitting at the kitchen table at home having a natter with her mum over a cup of tea as she told her about her day.

As she left the graveyard to return home, Grace felt lighter. Visiting the grave hadn't been as bad as she had feared; in fact, it had been cathartic in its own way. She left the looming belltower of St Brigid's church behind her and walked down the main street, calling into O'Herlihy's to pick up some fish pieces which Maggie had asked her to get so she could make a pie for dinner. Heavy rain was forecast for later, and they planned to hunker down by the fire for the evening.

When she had said goodbye to Mrs O'Herlihy, she stepped out of the shop and walked straight into a man who was entering at the same time.

'Oh, sorry,' she said, moving to one side.

'My apologies,' he said in a plummy accent as he stepped to the same side.

'Sorry.' Grace laughed once again as they did a dance to the left and right.

He laughed too. 'I'm going to go left. You do the same.'

'Phew!' Grace giggled as they finally stepped clear of one another. 'I had visions of us being stuck in a loop like that forever – you stepping left and me stepping right, then you stepping right and me stepping left...'

Suddenly his face clouded over. 'You remind me of someone,' he said, taking her in. His dark eyes were narrowed and intense, and Grace felt very self-conscious standing there under his gaze. She guessed he was in his late forties or early fifties. His wavy, raven black hair was longish and falling over his eyes and he wore green wellingtons, mustard corduroy trousers and a green wax jacket.

'I just have one of those faces,' Grace said dismissively.

'That sweater...' he said.

She followed his eyes down to the turquoise jumper she wore – the one that had belonged to her mother – beneath her puffer coat. She had thrown it on for comfort as much as warmth before she left the house.

'It was my mother's...' she said, pulling at the wool with her thumb and forefinger. The man was still staring intently at her, making her feel uncomfortable. He seemed to be caught in a trance.

Just then he reached his hand out towards her and for a moment, Grace thought that he was about to touch her. She was relieved when he stopped himself at the last minute.

'I'd better head on,' she said, making her way past him, keen for the awkward encounter to be over and to be on her way again.

'Wait!' he called after her.

She turned around. 'What is it?'

She watched his face as expressions flitted over it. It seemed as though he was about to say something, but then he changed his mind at the last minute. 'It's nothing, sorry...'

'Okay, bye,' she said and walked off, dodging the puddles that had formed along the path from the earlier rain.

'Yes, goodbye,' he called after her.

She continued along by the sea wall, where she stood for a moment to watch the foam-topped breakers as they rolled in off the Atlantic. Gulls swooped and scavenged the sand for creatures left behind by the tide. As she climbed up the grassy headland towards Maggie's cottage, she was still thinking about the strange man.

'How did you get on, love?' her aunt asked as she came into the kitchen a while later. Maggie was standing in front of her easel. She had started work on a seascape the day before, and Grace was fascinated to watch her aunt work. There was no denying her talent. Maggie seemed to instinctively know exactly where to add a dab of colour or a hint of shade, and suddenly a picture would start to appear before her eyes from what had been a blur of colours.

'I went to see the grave,' Grace admitted.

Maggie put down her paintbrush, giving Grace her full attention. She had recently dyed her frizzy curls a vibrant shade of purple. Grace had seen her with shocking pink and even blue hair before, but she had to admit that the purple suited her – it brought out the forget-me-not shade of her eyes.

'I haven't been able to face it myself. How was it?' Maggie asked.

As much as Grace missed her mum, she knew Maggie was grieving her sister too. Sometimes Grace would come into the kitchen to see Maggie holding the photograph of Rosa that usually sat on the dresser, tears glistening in her eyes. Grace would walk over to her and put her arms around her, and they would cling to one another, both feeling Rosa's loss so acutely. No words were needed; they knew the pain the other felt.

'It's still hard to believe that she's gone, but I chatted to her and told her how we were,' Grace said. 'It probably sounds silly, but it seemed as if she was with me.'

'It doesn't sound silly at all. It was just what you needed. Maybe I'll be able to talk myself into going in the next few days.' Maggie sounded wistful.

'By the way, I met the strangest man coming out of O'Herlihy's,' Grace said.

'Oh yeah?'

'He was awfully grand,' she said, putting on a posh accent. 'He was looking at my jumper in a daze – he said that I reminded him of someone.'

'Who on earth could that be?' Maggie cocked her head in puzzlement.

'I have no idea. It was so weird.'

'What did he look like?'

'He had black hair, and he was wearing a wax jacket and mustard coloured trousers.'

Grace was sure that Maggie's features darkened, then she quickly shook her head. 'Hmm, it's not ringing a bell. There are a few oddballs knocking around the village.'

'Anyway, I got the fish pieces in O'Herlihy's – will I start dinner?'

'That would be great, lovey,' Maggie said, picking up her paintbrush once more. 'I have to say, it's nice having you here. The company is good for me.'

'You might be stuck with me.' Grace sighed as she took out a pot and filled it with water from the tap. 'I don't know when I'll be ready to go home. I feel close to Mum here, but I'll need to think about getting a job at some stage. My savings won't last forever. Then I have Mum's house to think about. I'll need to face sorting that out eventually too.'

'There's no rush. All those things can wait a while. You'll always have a home here with me, Gracie.'

Every time she thought about the future and what she was going to do with her life, she felt a knot of panic pull a little tighter inside her. She knew she wasn't ready to return to Dublin, but she couldn't put it off indefinitely. And what was she going to do about a job? The thought of returning to accountancy filled her with dread. It was only since she had taken time out that she had realised she had been unhappy in her job for a while, but what else could she do? She had spent years studying to be an accountant, then working her way up the career ladder. She wasn't qualified to do anything else. Staying with Maggie in Inishbeg Cove was a balm to her wounded heart, but she couldn't avoid reality forever. She would have to make a decision about her future soon.

5

A few days later, Ruairí, Maggie and Grace were standing in the café looking towards the back wall, which acted as a gallery for Maggie's artwork. They were helping her to hang a new painting to replace one that had recently been sold.

'Hmm, maybe a little more to the right,' Grace suggested.

Maggie tilted the painting a fraction on her side. 'Now?'

'Up slightly,' Ruairí said.

Maggie did as instructed.

'Perfect,' Grace said and they stood back to admire the seascape. An abstract of blues and greens, it reminded Grace of the tumble of a wave.

Every few days Maggie and Grace would call into the café to check on sales with Ruairí. They would replace any pieces that had sold with newer artwork, or sometimes Ruairí would have the details of a customer who wanted to commission a piece from her. Then when they were finished, they would treat themselves to a coffee and generous wedge of cake.

'Two more sold yesterday, Maggie,' Ruairí announced.

'Will you slow down? I can't paint at the rate you're selling them!' Maggie joked.

'You'll have to start paying me commission.' Ruairí winked. 'Can I get you both a cuppa?'

'That would be lovely, thanks.'

Maggie and Grace took a seat at a table. After a few minutes Penny Murphy arrived with a pot of tea and two china mugs. She also gave them a slice of Ruairí's homemade apple tart.

'Penny, I don't think you've met my niece, Grace, properly. Grace, this is Penny Murphy,' Maggie said. She turned to Grace. 'Penny is giving Ruairí a helping hand here in the mornings.'

'Pleased to meet you,' Grace said, shaking Penny's hand across the table. Maggie had already filled Grace in on how Penny had recently left her husband, the famous artist Joe de Paor, and had returned to the village to mend her broken heart but had fallen in love with her old flame, Tadgh. Grace knew Tadgh from all the summers she had spent in the village, and had been shocked to hear he had been hit by a falling tree during a recent storm. He had been knocked unconscious and had been brought to hospital by air ambulance but miraculously, he had made a full recovery. Grace, her mum and Maggie had often gone to his restaurant as a treat for a birthday or if they had something to celebrate. Grace recalled with a pang of sadness that the last time they had gone there had been to celebrate Rosa finishing her first round of chemotherapy. How premature their celebrations had been.

'How's Tadgh doing?' Maggie asked, bringing a forkful of flaky pastry to her lips.

'He's doing great,' Penny said. 'He has recovered much faster than anyone expected. It's hard to believe he was in a coma just two months ago.' She laughed. 'He's itching to get back to the restaurant, of course.'

'When I heard about the accident, I thought he was a goner. It's a miracle he's still alive.' Maggie shook her head. 'I must say we've missed the place while it's been closed.'

'Well, I have some good news for you! He's having a little reopening party this Friday evening if you're around?'

'Oh, that sounds exciting. I'm glad he's finally on the mend. You can count us in,' Maggie said enthusiastically. 'Knowing Tadgh, he'll be back into the swing of things in no time.'

'You and I both know he won't stay out of trouble for too long.' Penny grinned. Grace noticed that her eyes shone as she spoke about the man she loved. Maggie had told her that Penny and Tadgh had been inseparable as teenagers, and it was nice to see that they had rekindled their romance.

'How's your little girl doing?' Maggie asked then.

'Lucy is doing great – she started in Josephine's playschool a few weeks ago and is loving it.'

'Glad to hear that. Make sure you tell Tadgh that I was asking for him, Penny,' Maggie said.

'I will, of course, Maggie. Now, I'd better get back to work.' Penny nodded towards the queue that had formed in front of the counter.

After they had finished their cake, Maggie and Grace said goodbye to Ruairí and Penny and left the café to go home. They were walking down the street when Grace cried, 'That's him!'

'Jesus, Grace, you set the heart crossways on me! Who is it?' Maggie asked, looking around her in bewilderment.

'The strange man with the jumper fetish.'

Grace watched the smile leave her aunt's face and her

eyes narrow to slits when she saw the man walking towards them.

'That's Patrick Cavendish,' Maggie said after a beat.

'Well, Patrick Cavendish has a thing for old cashmere sweaters,' Grace quipped.

'Are you sure that's the man you met, Grace?' she asked, her eyes never leaving him.

'I'm positive.' They watched from a distance as he stopped outside Sarah O'Shea's post office and dropped some letters into the mailbox that was built into the wall.

'So who is he?' Grace asked.

'He's one of the Cavendishes from Cavendish Hall out the road.'

'Is he a bit ... odd?' Grace asked.

'*Aragh*, he probably just got you confused with someone else.'

They watched as Patrick drew near to them.

'Good morning, Maggie,' he said as they walked past each other, then stopped dead. 'It's you – the one with the blue sweater,' Patrick said, staring at Grace as though he was caught in a trance again.

Grace elbowed her aunt. 'See, I told you!' she hissed under her breath.

'Patrick...' Maggie said tersely. She moved to walk past him, but he stood in her way, blocking their path.

'And this is?' he prompted Maggie.

'I'm Grace,' Grace said before Maggie could speak.

His eyes widened. 'Sh-she's your niece? Rosa's daughter?'

Maggie nodded. 'Grace is staying with me for a bit since her mother passed away,' she said stonily.

'I was ever so sorry to hear about that.' He seemed to

drift off into a reverie. 'She was ... wonderful. Please accept my condolences on your loss.'

Maggie grimaced. It looked as though she going to say something else, but Grace interrupted her. 'You knew my mum?' she asked. She loved hearing her mother brought to life. Maggie regaled her with stories about her mother from when she was younger, and Grace never tired of hearing them. 'Do you see that rock over there?' she would say. 'One year your mother and I lay sunbathing on it all day. We both fell asleep and were so sunburnt when we woke that we couldn't walk home.' She had only ever heard Maggie's stories, but here was a man who had known her mother too and Grace craved new anecdotes about her.

His eyes took on a faraway look. 'Well, we were...' he paused, as if to choose the right word, '...friendly when we were younger.'

'Right.' Maggie said, linking Grace's arm. 'Come on, Gracie, we'd better get going before it gets dark.'

Maggie tugged on her elbow and Grace felt a stab of disappointment. It wasn't like Maggie to be so rude. It seemed her aunt wasn't going to let her hear what Patrick had to say about her mum.

'Yes, of course. Goodbye, ladies,' Patrick said, standing aside to let them past. 'It was lovely to meet you, Grace.'

'Was my mum friendly with him?' Grace remarked to Maggie once Patrick was out of earshot. There was something familiar about Patrick Cavendish, as if she had met him before but couldn't place where. Perhaps she had bumped into him with her mother over the years, but she couldn't recall when. 'I don't think I ever heard Mum mention his name before.'

'Sure, you know what teenagers are like. Your mother was a good-looking young woman, and she had lots of admirers. He probably just knew her to see from around the village, that's all,' Maggie said dismissively.

Grace turned and watched the man – in a bottle-green wax jacket and wellingtons that looked as though they had seen better days – make his way down the path.

'Never mind him,' Maggie said, putting an arm around her shoulder and turning her around again. 'I think rambling around in his big old house on his own has sent him a bit cuckoo.'

As they started to walk back towards the cottage, unease washed over Grace. She had a feeling that there was more to this than Maggie was letting on. Something about Patrick Cavendish niggled at her, and a feeling deep within, told her that this wouldn't be the last she would see of him.

6

A rush of steam greeted Tadgh as he opened the oven door and lifted out the tray of bacon-wrapped scallops. He left them to cool before dashing across the kitchen to put the final touches to a tray of smoked salmon. His forehead was creased in concentration as he worked.

It was his reopening night and Penny could almost see the adrenaline coursing around his body as he worked: he came alive when he was in his kitchen. She loved his passion for his work: his attention to detail and high standards made his restaurant the best for miles around. Outside the kitchen door they could hear chatter and laughter as more guests arrived. Penny, who had offered to help out for the night, assembled a selection of hors d'oeuvres onto a tray and was glad to escape the heat of the kitchen as she went outside to greet their guests.

As she stepped out into the restaurant, the buzz of excited chatter rippled around between the vaulted caverns. They had pushed back all the tables and chairs to make standing room for everyone, and had hung lanterns along the walls so that the place was lit with soft, flickering candlelight. The restaurant was almost full, even though the party wasn't due to start for another ten minutes.

Penny moved around, greeting the villagers and offering them Tadgh's delicacies to sample. She had roped in Ruairí to help, and he was in charge of the drinks. He was working his way through the room, balancing a tray of champagne flutes in one hand and offering them to guests.

On the opposite side of the room Mrs O'Herlihy, the supermarket owner, was chatting to Jim from The Anchor and his wife, Maureen, who owned the B&B.

'Jim, Maureen, it's great to see you both,' Penny said, going over to greet them. 'Tell me, how are Greg and Sarah getting on?'

Greg and Sarah's newborn twins had spent several weeks in the Neonatal Intensive Care Unit. They had only recently been allowed to come home so, understandably, they weren't able to be here tonight.

'They're exhausted, as you would expect, but so thankful to have their babies at home where they belong at last. They had a rough few weeks travelling up and down to Limerick to see them, but the babies are thriving now. Greg has closed the ice-cream parlour for the winter months so the two of them are at home muddling through together.'

'Tell me, what did they call them?'

Maureen's face took on a wistful look. 'Della-Alice and Emily. Della-Alice was named after my late sister Della, who was Greg's birth mother, and Alice was his adoptive mother's name. Emily is named after Sarah's mother.'

Penny's mother Rita had told Penny the story of Greg's trip from North Carolina to Inishbeg Cove in search of his birth parents. He had managed to discover that Maureen's younger sister Della had been his birth mother, but she had died from postpartum complications not long after he had been born.

'Della-Alice and Emily – two beautiful names. I can't wait to meet them when they get a little stronger.'

'Oh, before I forget,' Maureen went on, 'Sarah asked me to thank Tadgh for the stews and casseroles he dropped in to her recently. She said it was the nicest thing to come home to good, hearty food after a long day in the NICU.'

Penny felt a rush of pride. 'Sometimes food is all we have to show people that we care. I'll be sure to pass on her thanks.' She hadn't known that Tadgh had done that. He was still thinking of other people even when he was recovering himself. 'I'd better go and hand some more of these out before they go cold.'

The door opened and she saw her parents arrive, holding hands with Lucy. Even though it would soon be her bedtime, Lucy had begged to be allowed to come to the party, so Rita and Pat had offered to bring her for an hour. When Lucy spotted Penny, she ran straight over and collided with her mother's legs. Penny had to hold the tray in both hands to stop it from toppling over.

'Hi, Mama!' Lucy sang.

'Hello, Lucy Lu, you look so pretty.'

Lucy began to twirl in her midnight blue organza dress that Penny had bought in Ballymcconnell especially for tonight.

'Ganny and Gandad said I can have a fizzy drink cos it's a special cassion.'

'Oh, did they now?' Penny raised her brows and rubbed her daughter's silky hair. 'Go on over to Ruairí, I think he might be able to find something for you.'

'Hi Mam, hi Dad,' Penny said to her parents. 'Lucy is

only here two seconds and she's gone looking for the fizzy stuff.'

'I wonder what could have put the idea in her head,' Rita said, feigning shock. Penny and her dad laughed.

'Great crowd,' Pat said as he helped himself to some hors d'oeuvres from her tray.

Across the room, Tadgh emerged from the kitchen doors. His smile spread right up to his eyes as he saw his thronged restaurant, and Penny knew he was in his element seeing it full with people once again.

'I'd better keep moving with these before the boss sees me chit-chatting,' Penny joked. She left her parents and made her way over to Tadgh.

'What a turnout,' she said, coming up beside him and surveying the crowd. Just then she noticed a well-dressed man – in his mid-fifties, she guessed, wearing a blazer and white shirt over jeans, standing alone in the corner. His face was tanned and his black hair was greying ever so slightly around the temples. He had a small notebook and he was writing something down in it. Penny watched him for a moment. She didn't recognise him from around the village. 'Who's that?' she asked Tadgh.

Tadgh followed her line of sight. 'I never saw him in my life. I don't think he's from Inishbeg Cove.'

'I wonder what he's writing?'

'Perhaps he is a journalist sent from one of the local papers?'

'Or maybe he's from the Michelin guide,' Penny teased.

'It better not be that lot again.' Tadgh groaned.

Penny laughed. She knew Tadgh had no interest in chasing Michelin stars. He had told her the story about an undercover inspector who had arrived from the prestigious guide to rate the restaurant a few years back. When Tadgh found out who he was, he turfed him out on his ear.

'I hate all that poncy stuff,' Tadgh complained. 'I just want to make good food and serve it to customers who appreciate it. I don't want people to come here because they want to be seen or they think they should because it has won an award. I like that we're this small restaurant that no one really knows about unless you're from the area or someone has told you about us. I don't want to lose that.'

'Well, why don't you go over and find out who he is?'

'All right,' Tadgh said, moving away.

Penny watched as he made his way across the room and began chatting to the man. They shook hands, but their brief chat was over almost before it had begun. Tadgh returned to her.

'Strange,' Tadgh muttered, shrugging when he reached her.

'So who is he?'

'Beats me! I went over and told him who I was, but he just said his name was Liam so I asked him if he wanted to ask me any questions or wanted any more information about the restaurant, but he looked at me as though I was mad. He didn't tell me anything about himself. Normally if a journalist or someone is sent from a paper to cover an event, they'll introduce themselves and tell you what paper they're from.'

'Hmm.' Penny was as puzzled as Tadgh. 'You should have just asked him out straight what he is doing here.'

'Well I didn't want to be rude...' Before they could dwell on it, though, a pair of arms were flung around him and he was pulled into a bear hug.

'There you are, Tadghy boy,' Maggie said, squeezing him tightly.

'Maggie!' Tadgh laughed. 'Thanks for coming.' He kissed her on the cheek.

'We're all just glad to have you back open again! Come here, you,' Maggie said, pulling him into another hug. Maggie had known Tadgh since he was a baby. She had babysat him when she was a teenager and retained a motherly affection for him even after all these years. When his parents had died in the horrific crash, Penny recalled that it had been Maggie who had stepped up and been the one to organise a rota to cook dinners and to help Tadgh with Senan.

'You know my niece, Grace, don't you?' Maggie continued, gesturing to the pale, willowy woman beside her.

'Of course, how are you doing?' Tadgh asked. They had met briefly at the funeral.

Grace nodded. 'I'm doing okay, thank you. Maggie is taking good care of me.'

'You remember Penny Murphy, don't you?' Tadgh gestured towards her.

'I do, of course – sure, don't I meet her every morning in Ruairí's place?' Maggie said, helping herself to some wafer-thin smoked salmon curled onto Guinness bread from Penny's tray. 'Don't tell me he's roped you into working here too?'

Penny laughed. 'It's just for tonight.'

'I hope he's paying you!' Maggie jerked a shoulder in the direction of the stranger, who was engrossed in writing in his notebook. 'Who's yer man?'

Tadgh shook his head. 'We were wondering the same thing.'

'Well, he's writing an essay, whatever he's at. Maybe he's a critic,' Maggie suggested.

'In that case, I'd better get to the reason we're all here.'

Tadgh put an arm around Penny's shoulder and kissed her head before clinking a spoon against a glass. Eventually a hush fell and the crowd waited for him to speak.

He cleared his throat before beginning. 'You're all very welcome here tonight – it's so good to be back! The reason I invited you all is that I wanted to thank you for your support over the years, but especially over the last two months. I'm very grateful to be surrounded by so many friends and family – it makes it all the more special. I have to say a very big thanks to my lovely Penny, who has been by my side throughout my recovery.' He turned to her. 'Penny, I wouldn't have got through it without you.'

Tears pushed into her eyes at his words.

'So tonight, I want to raise a glass to second chances.' Tadgh lifted his flute in the direction of his guests.

'To second chances,' the crowd chorused in return.

'Now eat, drink and be merry.'

As a round of applause broke out among the crowd, Penny reached up and kissed him on the cheek.

'What was that for?' he asked, smiling at her.

She grinned up at him. 'For just being you.'

7

A few days later Grace was running herself a bath, while Maggie stood in the kitchen chopping carrots to make a stew. The day had been wild and raging and after their swim, they had decided that a hearty meal and an evening by the fire was the only thing for it. Maggie browned the beef in the pan before tipping it into the pot to boil with some oregano and parsley, and it wasn't long before the cottage was scented with the herby aroma. She had begun to peel potatoes to go with the stew when there was a knock on the door. Wiping her hands on her apron, she went to answer it, and was stunned to see Patrick Cavendish standing on her doorstep. Of all the people it could have been, he was the one person she hadn't expected. She instantly thought back to the last time he had had the audacity to knock on this door. Her heart began to thump: had he already figured everything out?

'Patrick,' she said curtly. 'What can I do for you?' She stepped outside and pulled it shut behind her. Although Grace was in the bathroom, she could come out at any moment and Maggie didn't want her to see Patrick there.

She knew that her niece already had suspicions about the man, and if she saw him at the cottage, Maggie would have a hard time convincing her that nothing was going on.

'Maggie, I hope you will excuse the impromptu visit, but I wasn't sure how best to approach you...' he began.

'Well, you're here now. What is it?'

'Yes, well, you see, it's a matter requiring utmost discretion,' he continued, dancing around his words.

'Oh, spit it out, for heaven's sake, Patrick!' Maggie didn't have the patience for Patrick's politeness.

'Of course, Maggie,' he said, looking abashed. 'I'm sorry.' He took a deep breath and cleared his throat. 'I wanted to talk to you about your niece, Grace,' he began.

Her heart picked up speed. It was as she feared. 'Go on.'

'When I saw her down in the village wearing that turquoise sweater, I thought I was seeing things. I recall your sister wearing that exact sweater, and it was like a vision before me. For a moment, it was like looking at Rosa. I had to stop and give my glasses a rub. I thought perhaps I was seeing things, but then when I met her with you and you introduced me to her as Rosa's daughter, I knew I hadn't been imagining things.'

Maggie narrowed her eyes. 'And?'

'You know her mother and I had a ... relationship ... many years ago,' Patrick stammered.

'That was a long time ago,' she said dismissively. 'Look, Patrick, why are you here?'

'I would like to meet my daughter,' he blurted, finally mustering some backbone.

Maggie was stunned. He hadn't made contact with his daughter in almost thirty years and now that Rosa had passed away, he finally decided that he wanted to see her? Of course they had seen him around the village over the years but they had always given him a wide berth. It was one thing coming here and mentioning her recently deceased sister, but to try and lay claim to Grace after all these years too... the man had some neck. Fury warmed her veins. 'You've some cheek, Patrick Cavendish!' she said through gritted teeth. 'The poor girl has been through enough in recent weeks. How dare you?'

Maggie watched as his face fell. Was his life in that big old tumbledown mansion really so lonely that he was desperately searching for someone to connect with? But that was the Cavendish family for you, she thought bitterly: after years of being wealthy landlords with poor tenant farmers toiling their land, they thought they owned everything. They still had a sense of entitlement even though times had long since changed.

'I'm very sorry, Maggie, I don't want to upset anyone...' Patrick looked abashed.

'So stay away from her,' Maggie warned.

He lowered his gaze to the ground. 'Please accept my apologies, Maggie. You're right, my timing isn't the best. I'll leave you in peace.' He turned and walked away along the coast road.

Maggie was trembling with rage as she went back inside her cottage and closed the door behind her. She was thankful that Grace hadn't seen him. The man had some nerve. His timing couldn't have been worse. Poor Grace was grieving, she didn't need him causing her any more upset. Patrick Cavendish was bad news. Did he think that because his family had been powerful historically, he could still exert his influence around the village? Well, those days are over, sunshine, she thought as she peeled potatoes with vigour. Rosa would be turning in her grave to think the man she had once loved so deeply but who had betrayed her so coldly had turned up here now, trying to lay claim to the most precious thing she had. Maggie could not let that happen. It was her duty to protect Grace. Maggie had to be Rosa's voice when she was no longer with them to tell them herself. Maggie would not let Patrick Cavendish hurt her sister ever again.

8

In the café a few days later the coffee machine hissed and spluttered as Penny frothed milk to make a latte. When she was finished, she brought the coffee to the customer. As she made her way back towards the counter, she spotted Mrs Manning sitting by the window wearing her trademark siren red lipstick and sipping tea from her very own china teacup, which she kept in the café especially. Although she was well into her nineties and quite frail these days, she still stopped by Ruairí's every morning for a cup of tea. She was a popular figure around the village and always brought cheer to the place.

'Good morning, Mrs Manning,' Penny said, stopping at her table.

'Good morning, Penny, my dear.' Mrs Manning put her teacup down.

'How are you doing?'

'Well, I'm still here and that's a miracle in itself.' She laughed heartily.

'Stop that talk, Mrs Manning, you're only a young one.' Penny moved on to clear off a table that had just been vacated. She took the dirty crockery and a copy of the regional newspaper, *The Atlantic Times,* that had been left behind, and brought them into the kitchen. As she was loading the crockery into the dishwasher, Ruairí picked up the paper and began flicking through it.

'There's Tadgh,' he said, pointing at a page.

Penny left the dishwasher and came over. She looked over his shoulder and saw a grainy black and white photo of Tadgh making his speech at the reopening night. The headline beside the photo was: 'Second Chances for Tadgh O'Reilly?'

'Well what does it say?' Penny urged.

Ruairí began to read aloud. 'OK. It says: "Last Friday saw the gathering of what promised to be one of the finest events in the Inishbeg Cove social calendar, with the reopening night of eponymously named restaurant Tadgh's. When I arrived, a large crowd were already assembled. Based on the turnout alone, I was expecting quite a treat. Tadgh's has a reputation for homemade food using the best locally sourced ingredients, and it follows that when you use the finest ingredients, you should get the finest result. I eagerly waited for the tray to come in my direction. When it finally arrived, I selected smoked salmon sitting on a bed of Guinness bread. Unfortunately, despite my anticipation, I could describe it as mediocre at best. Hoping for a better experience, I then sampled one of Tadgh's bacon-wrapped scallops. Fished straight from the waters of the cove, I thought they must surely be the freshest found anywhere in the land. Perhaps my expectations were too high, because sadly the scallops didn't live up to the hype and this customer was left with a bitter taste (pardon the pun) in his mouth. It seems the theme of the evening was 'Second Chances', with Tadgh himself making a speech to thank his customers for their support, but after being served hors d'oeuvres worthy of a frozen food aisle, I'm not sure *I'll* be giving the restaurant a second chance."'

Penny's heart sank. She felt like she had been punched. 'Tadgh will be devastated. He cooks it all himself from scratch – absolutely nothing served last Friday night was from a freezer. I should know,' she said angrily.

'It's pure tripe,' Ruairí said. 'Who's the journalist that wrote the review?'

Penny looked at the by-line. 'They're calling themselves *The Undercover Critic*.'

'Hmm, too cowardly to put their name to it? Well, they'd better stay far away from my café!'

'I know they're entitled to their opinion, but they shouldn't be allowed a platform to damage the reputation of a restaurant like that. Local newspapers are meant to be supportive of small businesses, not tear them down. It's downright irresponsible!' Penny was livid.

'It's probably some upstart who's just landed their first job in the world of journalism trying to make a name for themselves. I wouldn't worry, Penny,' Ruairí reassured her. 'We all know how great Tadgh's food is.'

'Well, I won't be showing this to him. He's finally getting back to doing what he loves, and this is the last thing he needs to see.'

'I quite agree,' Ruairí said, folding down the newspaper. 'This...' – he stuck the newspaper in the recycling bin – 'is the only place for it.'

They both got back to work as the café began to fill up with customers, and soon Penny didn't have time to think about the nasty review as she ground coffee beans and served up lighter-than-air cakes.

It wasn't long before Tadgh arrived for his daily takeaway coffee on his way to the restaurant. Penny saw a rolled-up copy of *The Atlantic Times* beneath his arm and her heart sank. She knew he had seen it. Somehow she had hoped that she could protect him from it.

'Did you see this?' He slammed the paper down on the counter between them. 'It's a review of my reopening night.'

'I did, actually,' she admitted. 'Only just before you came in.'

'I can't believe it.' Tadgh opened the paper and studied the review once more. 'They said my food was frozen – that's the worst insult you could give a chef! The whole village has probably seen it – actually, the whole county!'

Penny winced.

'I dread to think how many customers I could lose over this,' he continued.

'Why don't you contact the paper and ask who this Undercover Critic is? Perhaps you could invite them back for a proper meal and show them just how great your restaurant is,' Penny suggested. 'They can't possibly judge the food based on a few canapés.'

'Yeah, maybe you're right,' Tadgh said, calming down. 'I'll see if I can find out more about the critic. I've been following restaurant reviews for years and this is the first time I've ever seen this name. Even when you can tell a reviewer didn't enjoy a restaurant they always try to be balanced and fair, but this has nothing nice to say whatsoever. It almost feels personal!'

'Don't take it to heart,' Penny soothed. 'Ruairí reckons it's probably some rookie journalist who has landed their first job and wants to make a name for themselves.'

'They're certainly doing that,' Tadgh muttered.

The door opened then and Maggie, Grace and the rest of

the swimmers came in. The group took their usual seats by the stove while Maggie came over to Tadgh.

'What's wrong, Tadghy?' she asked. 'You've a face that would stop a clock!' Damp curls peeped out from beneath her woollen hat.

'It's this bloody review,' Tadgh said, pointing at the newspaper.

'Give it here.' Maggie took it from his hands and began to read it. 'Ah, that's just nasty,' she said, shaking her head, after she had finished. 'We all know what your food is like. The cheek of them! They must have been at a different restaurant!'

Suddenly, Tadgh's eyes became animated. 'Do you think it was the man – you know, the one who spent the evening writing in his notebook?' he asked.

'It has to be,' Penny agreed, recalling the strange man standing alone in the corner.

'When I approached him and introduced myself, he still didn't tell me why he was there,' Tadgh said.

'I saw him too,' Maggie said. 'Very odd, he was. It looked like he was having a go at rewriting *Ulysses*.'

'Hmm, maybe I'll give the paper a call and see if they can shed any light on it.' Tadgh glanced at his watch. 'Anyway, I'd better head up to the restaurant and start taking my food out of the *freezer* for tonight's service,' he said sardonically, leaving the café with the newspaper folded under his arm.

9

A few days later, Grace sat down on the smooth flat rock in the centre of the cove and flicked open her sketch pad. She had always loved this rock. As large as a table and right in the centre of the cove, it commanded the best view of the horseshoe-shaped bay. Above her, clashing shades of indigo, coral pink and peachy oranges draped the sky. Being on the edge of the wild Atlantic Ocean, the sunsets over Inishbeg Cove were always spectacular. She could remember being a little girl and holding her mother's hand as the sun set. Rosa always told her to 'say goodnight to Mrs Sun', and Grace would obediently wave up at the sky as the neon red ball of fire slipped below the horizon for another day. Her heart snagged at the memory. She fished her pencil out of her backpack and began working quickly to get the layers of the streaked sky just right before the light was lost. Soon she became engrossed in her work, moving the pencil in small, deft movements.

'Did you know your mum used to sit in that exact spot sketching like that too?' a voice said suddenly.

Grace swung around to see Patrick Cavendish standing beside her. 'Oh, hi, Patrick,' she said, dropping her pencil and lowering her sketch pad, suddenly feeling self-conscious.

'Rosa would sit up there with her sketchbook staring out at the horizon. Nothing could break her focus when she had the charcoal in her hand.' He nodded towards Grace's sketch. 'That's good,' he said.

'Oh, it's very rough.' She quickly closed the sketchbook, embarrassed. She had always felt that her mother and aunt had got the lion's share of the creative genes. Although Grace could hold her own, she knew she didn't have a fraction of their talent. But sketching always helped to calm her mind whenever she was feeling stressed or worried. Her brain could concentrate on those small feather-light strokes and switch off from everything else careering around inside her head.

'You look very like her,' Patrick said. 'You've the same mannerisms.'

Grace was surprised; their likeness wasn't always obvious on first glance. Although she knew her facial features resembled her mother's, Grace's dark, straight hair was unlike her mother's mass of frizzy blonde curls.

'Did you know my mum well?' she ventured. The way Patrick spoke about her mother, it sounded as if he had known her very well indeed, which was at odds with what Maggie had told her.

He hesitated before speaking. 'I did, yes, at one time in our lives...'

'Were you in school together?' Grace tried again. He was being infuriatingly vague. It was as though he wanted to share something with her, but a force was holding him back.

'Sadly not.' He laughed. 'I was shipped off to boarding

school from the age of five, and of course your mother stayed here and went to the primary here in Inishbeg Cove, then secondary school in Ballymcconnell, but we got to know one another the summer we finished school, after being introduced at the village festival. We were both seventeen, if I remember correctly.' His eyes took on a wistful look. 'Your mum was a real firecracker. She was the life and soul of every party.'

Grace smiled as his words brought her mother to life. It was lovely to hear someone else reminisce about Rosa's joie de vivre back from a time before Grace was born. Rosa had had an energy about her that was irrepressible. Grace's heart constricted as she remembered her. 'She sure was,' she agreed.

'She was my first love,' he went on.

Grace was shocked. 'You – and my mum – were a couple?' she asked, doing her best to disguise her surprise, but knowing that she was failing miserably. Even though Rosa had been a very relaxed mother raising Grace and had far more liberal attitudes than some of her friends' mothers, Grace had never heard her mum talk about any boyfriends. For some reason, the topic was always a no-go area. Rosa had obviously had some kind of relationship – or perhaps it had been an encounter – with the man who was Grace's father but after that, as far as Grace knew, she had never had another relationship. So it seemed shocking to meet a man who was telling her that he had once been involved with her mother.

'Yes, for that summer and for a time afterwards we were inseparable. I know we were both so young, but I loved her very much.'

Grace's head was spinning; he was telling a completely

different story to Maggie. 'Why did you break up?' she asked, unsure whether she should believe him.

He frowned and his eyes clouded over. He shook his head. 'I'm afraid I've probably said too much.'

'Of course,' Grace said, abashed, knowing the moment was lost. She cursed herself for overstepping the mark with her questioning. Just as he was opening up to her about her mother, revealing another side to the woman that Grace had loved so much, she had gone and shut him down.

He pursed his lips. 'I'd best be off, Grace. I want to be home before nightfall.' He tipped his hat at her and continued along the cove.

Grace picked up her pencil and tried to finish off her sketch, but her head was all over the place. Why hadn't Maggie told her any of this? she wondered. Her head was teeming with questions and she knew it was futile trying to draw now, so she sighed heavily and began to gather up her belongings. It was getting late, anyway – dusk was falling and the last thing Grace wanted was to be making her way along the rambling boreen in the darkness.

As she powered over the bumpy path, questions tumbled over in her mind. Maggie had suggested that Rosa had hardly known Patrick, but according to Patrick they had been in a relationship. Who was telling the truth? But no matter how hard she tried, she couldn't imagine Rosa and Patrick together. They seemed an unlikely couple. When Grace looked at the photos of her mother as a teenager that Maggie had displayed on the shelves of the dresser in the cottage, she wore flares and a huge afghan coat over colourful tops. Her mother had always been quite bohemian, and Patrick seemed too strait-laced for her. Patrick Cavendish was very *proper* – she couldn't imagine him being attracted to someone as alternative as her mother had been back then and likewise, she couldn't see Patrick Cavendish being her mother's cup of tea either. But perhaps in his youth, Patrick had been different. After all, her mother, although she always dressed colourfully to the day she had died, had mellowed more in her tastes as she had got older and she wasn't as extroverted as she had once been.

As she ascended the headland towards Maggie's cottage, none of it sat right with Grace. She hated to doubt her aunt, who was like a second mother to her, but she couldn't help wondering if Maggie was being entirely truthful. And if she wasn't, then just what was she hiding?

10

Grace pushed the door open and entered the warm cottage. The peaty smell of the turf fire filled her nostrils, combined with the hearty aroma of the ham that Maggie had bubbling on the Aga. Maggie was a fantastic cook. Ever since Grace was small she had loved her aunt's dinners, but today her appetite seemed to have left her.

'There you are, love,' Maggie said. 'I was getting worried about you. I don't like you walking along that road in the dark.'

Grace walked over to the fire that was smouldering in the grate and warmed her hands over it.

'Dinner won't be long now, I've made ham with parsley sauce and mashed potato,' Maggie said. 'I know it's one of your favourites. I've an apple and blackberry crumble in the oven for dessert too, so I hope you're hungry.' Maggie stirred a pot. 'So did you do any sketching?'

Grace remained silent.

'Is everything okay, Grace?' Maggie turned around from

the Aga. Usually Grace would fill her in on who she'd met or what she'd seen on her walks to and from the village.

'I met Patrick Cavendish down in the cove.' The words seemed to tumble from Grace's mouth like bullets.

'I see,' Maggie replied, placing the wooden spoon down on the worktop and giving Grace her full attention. She folded her arms across her chest. 'And what did he have to say for himself?'

'He said that he and my mum had gone out together once upon a time...' Grace began.

'That fella!' Maggie spat, her features arranging themselves into an annoyed look. 'They probably kissed once or twice, but it was nothing more than that.'

'He said she was his first love,' Grace countered.

'Honestly, Grace, the man isn't all there.' Maggie shook her head in exasperation as she began stirring the pot once more.

But Grace couldn't let it lie. Something about Maggie's behaviour told her there was more to this. Her story had already changed. Maggie had denied that Rosa even knew Patrick, and now she was admitting that they may have kissed.

'Maggie,' Grace begged. 'Please be honest with me.'

Panic flitted across Maggie's features. 'Oh, Grace, what do you want to go digging up the past for? Think of your poor mother – she would hate this!'

'I know, Maggie, but I have to know. For years I never heard her talk about a man, let alone who my father might be. Don't you think that's odd?'

Maggie shrugged. 'She had her reasons.'

'Please, Maggie, I've just buried my mother and I feel so lost. I want to know the truth.'

'I can't. I can't do it to Rosa...' Maggie said determinedly.

'And what about me?'

'What about you? It's none of your business what your mother did or who she went out with before you were born!' Maggie was dogged.

Grace took a deep breath. The words she had wanted to say for so long but that always seemed to clog in her throat bubbled up and spilled out. 'I need to know the truth. Who is my father, Maggie?' she demanded.

Maggie's hands fluttered to her throat and her whole face was etched in pain. Grace could see her aunt wrestling with what to do as though there was an invisible force inside, tearing her apart. Grace held her breath as she watched her aunt. There was no way back from here. Grace knew this was difficult for Maggie; she could see that she was torn, but she held the answers to Grace's past. If she wasn't prepared to tell the truth, Grace didn't like to think about the damage it would do to their relationship. She didn't think she would ever be able to forgive Maggie if she didn't give her the answers that she so desperately needed. Her mother had taken her secrets to her grave with her, and now the decision rested squarely with Maggie.

Maggie's shoulders sagged, as if she had finally given up the battle. She opened her mouth to speak and Grace's heart thumped in her chest.

'Patrick Cavendish is your father,' Maggie began.

Even though Grace had somehow suspected this might be true, the words still hit her like a train. Her head started to spin and her legs were weak. She had spent her whole life wondering who her father might be and now that she had the truth, she didn't think she was ready for it.

Her knees started to buckle.

'Oh no, you don't.' Maggie hurried over and grabbed her just before she fell. 'Here, sit down.' She guided Grace into an armchair and encouraged her to put her head down between her knees.

Grace's vision was blurred and the blood pulsed loudly in her ears. She had been the same way her whole life: whenever anything shocking happened, she always felt faint.

'Are you okay?' Maggie asked after a few minutes. 'Take a deep breath.'

'Sorry, it's just the shock,' Grace mumbled.

'You're okay, love, take your time,' Maggie soothed. 'It's a lot to take in. Why don't I make us both a cup of sweet tea? And then when you're feeling up to it, I'll fill you in on the whole story...'

11

Maggie placed the steaming mug in Grace's hands and sat down beside her on the sofa. She looked at her niece's wan face. Her expression was etched with pain, and she seemed to have the weight of the world on her shoulders. Even though she knew the time had come to tell Grace the truth, guilt was weighing her down. Maggie was about to reveal her late sister's secrets. She just hoped that if Rosa was looking down on her right now, she would be able to forgive her.

Since Rosa's death, Maggie had been terrified of this moment arriving. She realised that Grace needed to know the truth, but Maggie also wanted to be loyal to her sister's memory. She was torn. Rosa had always been adamant that she didn't want Grace to have anything to do with her father, and Maggie had respected her wishes. Why hadn't she brought up the conversation with Rosa before she died? she kept asking herself. She should have asked Rosa what her wishes were, but now she was flailing around in the void left behind by her sister, hoping she was doing the right thing. She could hardly blame Grace; the poor thing was feeling forlorn with the loss of her mother. Didn't Grace have a right to know the truth after all these years? She just wanted a connection; it was only natural that her mother's death would bring the old feelings and questions about who her father was to the fore once more. Maggie had been wrestling with her conscience ever since Grace had started asking questions, but now she knew the time for honesty had come.

'Thanks, Maggie,' Grace said, taking the mug from her and curling her slender fingers around its warmth.

'Are you feeling okay now, love?'

Grace nodded. The dizziness had subsided and her heart rate had slowed again. 'I want you to tell me everything.'

'Okay then, I suppose I'll start at the beginning.' She laughed nervously and Grace smiled encouragingly at her aunt. 'When your mother was seventeen she met Patrick Cavendish at the village festival. The Cavendish family were big Protestant landowners here for hundreds of years, and would have employed many of the villagers on their estate either in service in the big house or on the farm. Your grandmother worked in the kitchen there for a bit before she got married. Patrick was the eldest son, and the heir to the Cavendish estate. He was friendly with Donie Fahey, whose father managed the farm for the family, and Patrick had come along to the festival with him. When Donie introduced us to Patrick, I'll never forget how much he stood out.' A wry smiled formed on Maggie's lips. 'This was Ireland in the late eighties, so while the rest of us were wearing cut-off denim shorts and T-shirts, he was wearing a pair of corduroy trousers with a maroon long-sleeved shirt, even though it was the height of summer. For all his family's money, the knees in his pants were threadbare! The

Cavendish family didn't normally get involved much in village life; they always kept themselves to themselves, but Patrick was different. You could see he didn't have a superiority complex like his parents had, he just wanted to fit in. Anyway, we were all friendly to him but I could see that Patrick was taken with your mother. Oh, she was a looker in those days, Gracie,' Maggie said, as the corners of her lips turned up wistfully, 'but she was also charismatic and fun to be around. All the boys loved her. I remember feeling sorry for the poor lad because I thought he hadn't a snowball's hope in hell with her.' Maggie paused for breath. 'From that day on, Patrick became a fixture in our little group. And as he began to relax more and let his guard down, we discovered that he was actually good fun and not at all stuffy, like we had expected. We were all surprised to find that when you ignored the toff exterior and the shabby clothing, he was just like us. He began dressing more casually too when he hung around with us, and although he never wore jeans, he would wear a T-shirt with his trousers instead of a shirt.' Maggie took a sip of her tea before continuing. 'That summer we were all talking about our plans for September. I was in second year in art college so I was going back to Limerick to finish my degree, and your mother was talking about her plans to study teaching in Dublin. Patrick, though, always looked like he had the weight of the world on his shoulders whenever we had a conversation about the future. As the eldest son in his family, he knew he would inherit the estate whether he wanted to or not. His training under Donie Fahey's father had already begun, and he was resigned to the fact that his life was already mapped out and there would be no university for him.

One night we were sitting around a bonfire on the beach, when I noticed that Patrick and Rosa were deep in conversation. I think it was getting to him that he wouldn't have a chance to pursue his own studies. He wanted to be a pilot but his parents said there was no need to waste his time learning to fly when he would be inheriting the estate. From that night on, Patrick and Rosa grew close. Whenever we were in a group, the two of them always seemed to be huddled together talking, but it still came as a surprise when they kissed one night.' Maggie looked at Grace, who was transfixed by the story. 'I would never have picked him for your mother, and likewise, I wouldn't have chosen your mother for Patrick, but maybe that was what they liked about one another. Patrick was the opposite of Rosa and I think that perhaps she was a breath of fresh air to him.

Anyway, September came and we all went off to college, but Patrick had to stay behind in the village to learn how to be the country squire,' Maggie said dryly. 'Rosa would meet up with him, though, whenever she came home at the weekends. Whereas I thought college life might dampen her feelings for Patrick, it seemed absence made the heart grow fonder and their relationship went from strength to strength.

Then at Christmas-time, Rosa came home to the cottage looking pale. She was withdrawn. For the first time in her life, her spark was missing. I knew something was up with her. When I asked her what was wrong, she confessed that she had discovered she was pregnant. I asked her if it was Patrick's, and she just nodded, tears filling her eyes.

I assured her that everything would be okay, and asked when she was due. She said June. I told her that it wasn't ideal, with her being in her first year of college and everything, but she could still sit her exams in May then take the summer off to have the baby. She could be back in college in September if she wanted, or she could defer for a year if it was all too much. Ireland was a more progressive country by then – there were more options for women who had babies before marriage compared to even a decade before. Some colleges even had crèches. As you know, our parents had both passed on by then so I promised her I would be by her side every step of the way.

She was upset because this wasn't how she had planned things. I asked when she was going to tell Patrick and she told me that she was meeting him that night.'

'So, what did Patrick say when she told him?' Grace asked, riveted by the story of how she came to be.

'Well, according to your mother, Patrick was every bit the gentleman she had expected him to be. Although he was surprised, she had said that he actually seemed excited by the news. He told Rosa that he would speak to his parents about them marrying, if that was what she wanted, and she said yes. The estate had a dower house that had been lived in by his late grandmother that was lying empty, and the plan was to live in it after they married, so they wouldn't need to be under his parents' roof.'

'So what happened?' Grace asked, her eyes were as wide as saucers. 'Where did it all go so wrong? It sounded like they both loved each other and wanted to make it work.'

'Mr and Mrs Cavendish were not happy at all at Patrick's announcement. He didn't even tell them that Rosa was pregnant, only that he wanted to marry her. According to Rosa, he was trying to sort things out with them but he completely misread the situation. Oh, they were awful by all accounts, Gracie… They accused Rosa of trying to get her hands on his money – the cheek of them! She was a Catholic too, which didn't help matters. Although attitudes to religion had changed a lot in Ireland by this time, they were from a different generation. They were old-fashioned snobs and didn't think Rosa a suitable match for their son.'

'What did Patrick do then?' Grace asked, an uneasy feeling washing over her.

'According to Rosa, he was distraught. They discussed whether he should just walk away from them, but she didn't want to be responsible for a rift in his family. If he hadn't been the heir to the estate, it might have been easier, but being the first-born son came with heavy responsibility. Rosa told me that Patrick was keenly aware that generations of Cavendish men had had to make sacrifices for their family. I think Patrick really hoped that he might be able to persuade his parents, over time, so he asked Rosa to be patient. They were both in a right quandary about it all.'

'It sounds awful.' It was so difficult to listen to this story of heartbreak and forbidden love and know it was all because of her.

'It was a tough time all right, but Rosa was hopeful that everything would work out. Then one day Mrs Cavendish arrived here at the cottage with this girl called Tabitha standing beside her and Rosa invited them in. Before they had even sat down, Tabitha was crying, saying that she and Patrick were a couple and that she had just learnt that he was betraying her with Rosa!'

'Did they know she was pregnant?' Grace was aghast.

Maggie shook her head. 'No, I don't think so. She wasn't showing at that stage so I doubt they even realised.'

'So what did my mum do then?' Grace asked horrified, her earlier sympathy for Patrick had rapidly vanished. 'How could he have done that to Mum and to Tabitha?'

'Rosa was stunned at first, then angry. We all saw another side to Patrick that day,' Maggie said through gritted teeth. 'She realised that Patrick had been making a fool of her, stringing her along with false promises. She wrote to him and told him to never darken her door again. She cut off all contact, she refused to see him and she wouldn't take his calls. She went back to Dublin and worked hard at her studies – and lo and behold, she was in her flat a few weeks later, reading the *Irish Times*, and what should she see? Only an engagement notice from Mr and Mrs A. Cavendish announcing the engagement of their son, Patrick, to a Ms Tabitha Montgomery.'

'No!' Grace cried out in shock. She tried to imagine how distraught her pregnant mother must have felt reading those words inked in a newspaper column for the whole world to see. 'So it was true? Patrick was already in a relationship when he met my mother?'

'Yes.' Maggie shook her head sadly. 'Clearly Patrick patched things up with Tabitha and they arranged a wedding in record time. It seemed his parents felt she was a more suitable bride to be by his side as he took on the estate.'

Grace's heart fell. 'So what did he do?' she asked, knowing the answer before she had even asked the question. She knew how the story ended.

'Well he left Rosa high and dry, didn't he?' Maggie cried, unable to disguise her anger even after all these years.

'Even though he knew she was pregnant?' Grace was disgusted.

'Even though he knew she was pregnant,' Maggie repeated, hammering home the betrayal.

'Oh, Maggie,' Grace cried, feeling tears in her eyes as she thought about what her mother must have gone through.

'Come here, love.' Maggie threw her arms around her.

Grace realised then why her mother hadn't wanted to tell her who her father was; she hadn't been able to. She had been too heartbroken by Patrick's betrayal. She had clearly never got over it. 'Is that why she didn't tell me?' Grace asked quietly.

Maggie nodded. 'She was still hurt about it even after all these years. When she was dying, I didn't want to upset her by bringing it up again. I thought she might have told you before she passed away, but I think it was still too painful for her. I'm sorry, Grace. I know you just wanted answers, but can you see why it was hard for her to tell you the truth? He had the nerve to come sniffing round here the other day telling me that he wanted to get to know you, so I ran him out of here.'

'Patrick came here?' Grace was shocked.

'Yes, the other day when you were in the bath,' Maggie admitted.

'I see,' Grace said. 'So he knows I'm his daughter?'

Maggie nodded. 'He does. I told him to leave. Patrick Cavendish is bad news. He didn't just break your mother's heart; he broke *her*. I rallied around her and tried to help her through it as best I could, but it took her a long time to recover. Your mother had always been a wild child, but she was a shadow of her former self after Patrick jilted her. Her confidence never recovered. The gossip-mongers had a field day of course but Rosa kept her head held high. She continued her studies, even though it wasn't easy being a pregnant student. She sat her exams while heavily pregnant, then she came home here a few weeks before you were due. Would you believe, she went into labour on the same day that he got married at Cavendish Hall?'

Grace gasped. It seemed unimaginably cruel to think of her poor mother caught in the grip of contractions while Patrick celebrated his marriage.

'She was besotted with you when you arrived, Grace,'

Maggie went on, 'and I was glad to see a little of her spark begin to return. She channelled all her energy into being the best mother she could be, but she never opened her heart to another man again.'

Finally it all made sense: her mother's refusal to talk about her father, the pain in her eyes whenever Grace tried to raise the subject. It was because Patrick had caused her unbearable pain. Grace understood why she had closed her heart to love after Patrick. She stood up. 'I need to talk to him.'

'Why? I've told you everything you need to know,' Maggie countered.

'I feel I owe it to my mother,' she blazed. 'I want him to know what he did to her!'

'Just let it be, Grace. Don't go getting yourself upset. He's not worth it.'

Grace shook her head. 'No, he can't get away with it! I feel like I'm going to explode. I want to have it out with him.'

'Oh, Gracie, do you really think that's a good idea, love?' Maggie tried to reason with her.

'No, it's probably a terrible idea,' she agreed. 'But I'm going.' She went over to the coat stand and reached for her coat.

'You can't go now; it's far too late.' Maggie followed her. 'Please at least wait until the morning. If you still feel the same then, I won't stop you.'

'All right.' Grace sighed as she sat back down. 'But Patrick Cavendish won't know what's hit him when I'm finished with him.'

12

It was close to midnight when Penny eventually heard Tadgh's key in the front door. She had tucked Lucy up in bed several hours ago and had spent the evening watching TV by herself, waiting for him to come home from the restaurant. Although he was meant to be easing himself back into things, he had jumped straight back into work since the reopening night. It was like he had never been away from the kitchen.

'I thought you were supposed to be taking it easy!' Penny chided when Tadgh came into the living room. He looked exhausted. Dark circles shadowed his eyes. She knew that he was glad to be back in the restaurant again, doing what he loved, but she didn't want him overdoing it. He had had a large group booked in that evening so he was under pressure, but the last thing she wanted was for him to set back his recovery.

'You waited up for me?' He flopped down beside her on the sofa and kissed her forehead. The embers of the dying fire smouldered in the grate.

'Of course I did.' She snuggled in beside him. She could

smell a faint hint of the aftershave he had put on that morning. 'How was your day?'

Tadgh exhaled heavily. 'Terrible.'

She pulled back to look at him properly. 'Why? What happened?' Tadgh had been downhearted ever since he read the review of his reopening night in *The Atlantic Times*. He had called the editor, who had admitted that the review wasn't written by one of their employees but had been sent in anonymously via the email address theundercovercritic@gmail.com. Eager to fill space in the newspaper, he had published it. He apologised profusely and agreed that, with hindsight, it had been poor editorial judgement on his part and that it wasn't in the newspaper's usual spirit of supporting local businesses and community endeavours, and it should never have been printed. Straight away Tadgh had contacted the email address given to him by the editor, but he had received no response. He had googled 'The Undercover Critic' but couldn't find any other reviews written by the person, leaving him to wonder who this anonymous critic was and why they had chosen his restaurant as their first and only review.

'Remember that party of thirty I was telling you about that were booked in for tonight?' Tadgh went on.

'Uh-huh,' Penny said.

'They cancelled at the last minute,' he said bitterly.

'They did not!' Penny was shocked.

'I had turned down so many other reservations to cater for that group, so the restaurant was half-empty for the night. I had the full team in the kitchen with nothing to do.'

'Oh Tadgh, I'm sorry,' Penny said.

'They must have read the review,' Tadgh continued. 'Why else would they cancel so late in the day?'

'Well, there could have been lots of reasons,' Penny

reasoned. 'It's just unfortunate that people don't understand the effect these things can have on a small business.'

'But it gets worse...'

'Go on,' Penny urged, dreading what he might say next.

'A letter arrived from the Health Service Executive today. They are investigating a case of food poisoning that is alleged to have occurred in my restaurant!'

'Oh, Tadgh!' She gasped, knowing how serious this could be for his business.

'In all my time in the kitchen, I've never had one case of food poisoning,' Tadgh said. 'I sample all the food myself: the team and I eat whatever is on the menu for dinner. If there was something wrong with the food, we'd all have food poisoning too.'

'So what happens now?'

'They want to carry out an investigation, part of which will involve an inspection by a health official. Well, they can pull the place apart if they want, but I've nothing to hide. I'm proud of my restaurant and my team; they won't find any hygiene issues in my kitchen,' he said resolutely.

'But a person could have a dodgy stomach and blame it on what they ate in the restaurant, even though it might be nothing to do with the food at all. It's so unfair,' Penny said.

'Tell me about it.' Tadgh groaned. 'It's going from bad to worse. I put my heart and soul into that place. Ever since I took over the reins at eighteen, I've worked hard to make sure it kept to the standards my parents were known for. Now it feels as though I'm letting them down.'

Penny reached for his hand. 'Oh, Tadgh, come on, don't be so hard on yourself. Do you think it could be malicious?'

Tadgh looked shocked. 'You think it could be a fake report? But why would anyone do that?'

'It seems a bit coincidental, doesn't it? First there was the anonymous review and then this. Maybe someone's got it in for you,' Penny reasoned.

'Like who?'

'You don't think it could be Joe, do you?' Penny suggested, feeling guilty for even considering that her ex-husband, from whom she had recently separated, would be capable of doing something like this, but he was the only person she could think of who might harbour a grudge against Tadgh.

'I don't know, Penny.' Tadgh shook his head. 'Maybe it's me – maybe I just don't have what it takes any more. Maybe the accident took more out of me than I realised. Perhaps I'm not as good as I used to be.'

'That's nonsense, Tadgh, and you know it. We'll get to the bottom of it, I promise you,' Penny said, squeezing his hand.

13

The next morning Grace marched between the pair of acorn-topped piers that marked the imposing entrance to Cavendish Hall. Maggie had tried to talk her out of going yet again, but Grace had dug her heels in. Sleeping on it hadn't lessened her anger towards Patrick, as Maggie had hoped, and instead she had woken with renewed purpose. She was determined that he listen to what she had to say. Fury quickened her pace as she made her way up the avenue. She barely had time to take in the pretty gate lodge with its leaded windows, which looked as if it had been taken straight from an illustration in *Hansel and Gretel*. She continued along the avenue, which was guarded by majestic oak trees, gnarled and knotted with age. A carpet of russet leaves, left behind by the autumn winds, had gathered beneath their boughs. On either side of the avenue, fields springy with moss, where cattle chomped on luscious grass, rolled down towards the sea.

She had been walking for almost ten minutes, following the avenue as it snaked along, and there was still no sign of Cavendish Hall. She could have taken her car, but she had wanted to walk. She needed the time to gather her thoughts and think about what she was going to say to Patrick once she arrived.

Grace rounded a bend and suddenly a magnificent, two-storey Georgian mansion – the seat of the Cavendish family for generations – came into view. It was even more impressive than she had expected. The house had a single-storey wing on either side and a portico framed with four tall pillars in the centre. Two stone lions kept watch on either side of the door. Although Grace had heard about the grandeur of Cavendish Hall over the years, she hadn't been prepared for this. It was hard to believe that according to Maggie, Patrick lived all alone here in a house of this size.

Grace headed through the pillars and climbed the limestone steps where the soft stone had worn down in the centre from years of feet stepping over them. She rolled her shoulders back, took a deep breath, then rapped the large brass knocker against the timber door where black paint was peeling off. Suddenly Grace began to doubt herself. What the hell was she doing wasting her time coming here? Patrick had betrayed her mother so cruelly; nothing she said or did now would ever change that. But she needed to have it out with him, for her mother's sake; Patrick needed to realise what he had done.

It felt like she was waiting there for an age for someone to answer. She was about to turn and leave, guessing that Patrick wasn't at home, when she finally heard the heavy door creak open. She turned around to see Patrick standing framed in the doorway. He was wearing a tweed jacket, even though he was indoors.

'Grace?' he said, looking shocked. 'I-I'm sorry … sometimes I don't hear the door if I'm at the back of the house. Would you like to come in?'

It was mind-bending to realise that the man standing before her was her father; his blood ran through her veins. After years of wondering who he was, she had finally found him.

'Yes,' she said, feeling anger at his actions all those years ago rise within her once again.

She followed him inside to a walnut-panelled hall where a double staircase led up to a balcony that ran around the upper floor. The air smelled musty and damp, and the flagstones were covered in tatty Persian rugs. Light flooded through the stained-glass atrium. When she looked up, she saw that intricate plasterwork decorated the ceiling surrounding it. This was just the entrance foyer, and it was gigantic. She could picture this place in its glory days. She could almost hear the whinny of horses as elegant guests stepped out of carriages, draped in furs, anticipating an evening of fine food and merriment in Cavendish Hall. It must have been spectacular.

'Welcome to Cavendish Hall,' he said as she took in her surroundings. 'Will we go into the drawing room?'

Grace followed him through a set of mahogany double doors into a large room with green and gold chintz-covered furniture and a writing bureau. A lavish gilded chandelier hung from the ceiling and stern portraits of generations of the Cavendish family – *her ancestors* – looked down on her. Although a fire was burning in the grate, the room was still chilly, and she could see why Patrick wore his jacket inside the house.

'Sit down,' he offered. 'Can I get you something to drink?'

'A cup of tea would be good, thank you,' she said. Her heart was thumping wildly as she thought of the conversation that lay ahead.

Patrick disappeared to make the tea, leaving Grace looking around the drawing room. Maggie's entire cottage was the size of this room. She noticed the wallpaper was peeling in places and a thick layer of dust sat on the curtains. In the corner a blue plastic bucket sat beneath a leak, catching drops falling from the ceiling, but although the place was run down, there was no disguising its beauty.

Patrick returned a few minutes later with a teapot and two delicate china cups balanced on a silver tray. Grace realised that the days of servants in Cavendish Hall must be long over.

'I have to say I wasn't expecting to find you there when I opened the door,' Patrick began tentatively as he set the tray down and began to pour the tea.

'Maggie told me the truth,' Grace blurted, not wanting to waste time on pleasantries. She needed to offload what she had come to say. 'She said that you are my father.'

The room seemed heavy with silence as Patrick processed Grace's words. She waited for what felt like an eternity for him to speak.

'I always hoped this day would come,' he said eventually, as he set the teapot down. Grace was stunned to see tears fill his eyes.

'I knew as soon as I saw you in the street wearing your mother's old sweater that you were my daughter. I've waited so long for this moment.'

'I spent my whole life not knowing who my father was,' Grace said, taken aback by his display of emotion. 'It was only when you acted so strangely when we met that I began to have suspicions. I begged Maggie to tell me the truth, and she told me it was you.'

'You mean, your mother never told you?' Patrick sounded shocked.

Grace shook her head. 'She would never talk to me about it. I know now that she couldn't. You broke her heart, Patrick.'

He hung his head.

'Why did you do that to her?' Grace blasted. 'How could you treat my mother like that?'

He lifted his head. 'B-but she didn't want to be with me, Grace. She told me that herself.'

'What do you mean?' Grace asked, suddenly feeling unsure of herself.

'I loved your mother with all my heart, and I thought she loved me too until a letter arrived here out of the blue one day telling me that it was all over between us and that I wasn't to contact her ever again. I was shocked. One minute we were planning our future together – we were to have a child, and hoped to wed – then the next minute she didn't want to know me. Of course I tried to see her to find out what had changed, but she wouldn't talk to me.'

'That was because she found out that you were cheating on her with Tabitha!' Grace spat.

Patrick's mouth fell open. 'No! Whatever gave you that idea? Tabitha and I only became a couple after your mother told me that she didn't want to be with me any more.'

'But your mother and Tabitha went to Maggie's cottage! They told Mum that you and Tabitha were together—'

Patrick was aghast. 'My mother?' he said in disbelief. 'My mother called over to Rosa – with Tabitha?' He sat forward in his chair, gripping the arms fiercely. 'Are you sure, Grace?'

'I'm certain. Maggie told me the full story. My mother was heartbroken.'

Pain filled Patrick's face. 'It all makes sense now – why Rosa cut off contact with me so suddenly. I can't believe they were so manipulative.'

'What do you mean?' Grace wasn't following him.

'Rosa was the only woman I ever loved. I would never have betrayed her with another woman, and certainly not with Tabitha Montgomery. Tabitha and I had known each other from childhood. Our parents were friendly and we grew up together. I wasn't remotely attracted to her, yet my parents were not so subtle in their attempts to push us together. I knew Tabitha had always had feelings for me, and our parents hoped we might couple up, but I never felt the same way about her, no matter how hard they tried to persuade me that she was a good match. Money was growing tight for my family, and Tabitha's family were wealthy. By that time, we had had to sell off some of our land and let staff go. Although they never said so outright, I assume my parents hoped that Tabitha could help to save Cavendish Hall. My father told me it was my duty to wed according to my parents' wishes. It's hard to explain it now, because today it just sounds pathetic, but in a family like ours, being the eldest son came with a huge burden of responsibility. I was primed to take on this estate from the moment I could walk. There was never any other option for me. I remember my father leading me around the grounds when I was no more than three or four years old, telling me the names of all the fields, showing me every hillock and ditch and where the streams flowed. We were raised by nannies, then sent away to boarding school at a young age, only coming home at half-term or for the summer holidays, so I wasn't particularly close to my parents. I only realised when I got older, that my upbringing was very different compared with other children,' he said sadly. 'I was always so fearful of disrespecting their wishes. Growing up, my brothers were jealous of me being the eldest son, but how I envied their freedom. They could go to university and make careers for themselves without being stuck with this *noose* around their neck.' Patrick flushed with emotion. 'My father scoffed at the idea of marrying for love. Feelings were never important; the estate had to come first. Nothing could get in the way of that. He told me he had done the same with my mother. Marrying for love wasn't an option. It had to be strategic. I felt a sense of duty to uphold the family seat, but the idea of marrying for money abhorred me, and I told them this. And then I met Rosa, and knew she was the only woman I could ever love.'

His whole face softened when he mentioned her mother's name. 'When I told them that I wanted their permission to marry her, they were horrified and refused me outright. They wouldn't even consider the idea. My father asked if I wanted to be the person who lost Cavendish Hall after hundreds of years in the family. I hadn't even told them she was pregnant – I thought it best to hold off on that news until we got over the first hurdle – but he made it very clear to me that, if I wanted to save the estate, then marrying Tabitha was my only option. So they must have planned it together – my mother and Tabitha – as a way to get me to marry her,' he said angrily. 'My mother could be very manipulative, but for Tabitha to play a role in the deceit, just so she could get her way, is disgusting. No wonder Rosa ended our relationship so abruptly if she thought I was seeing Tabitha...' He held his head in his hands, clearly distraught. 'What must poor Rosa have thought? For all these years, I believed that she had fallen out of love with me.'

'But you make it sound like it was the Victorian era – that you had no choice but to follow your parents' orders and get their permission to be with my mum,' Grace countered. 'You were a grown adult and it was the late eighties!

The days of arranged marriages were long gone. Why didn't you just walk away from them all? You and Mum could have made your own life together without them. Why were you waiting for their approval?'

'When you say it like that, it sounds so simple, doesn't it?' He smiled sadly at her. 'It is my single biggest regret. The prospect of walking away from everything I knew – my whole life – was daunting. I had no college education, I had never had a proper job; Cavendish Hall was all I knew. How would I provide for Rosa and a child? I had no income to rent or buy a house for us to live in. I really thought that, with time, I could convince my parents to change their mind and accept Rosa as my wife. I was sure that once they met her and saw the woman I had fallen in love with, she would win them over.' His face clouded over. 'Then one day that letter was waiting for me from Rosa, stating that it was over. There was no explanation, just that she didn't want me to contact her again. Of course, I went to see her, to find out what was going on, but she refused to see me. She went back to college in Dublin and wouldn't take my calls, and my letters were always returned unopened. One day I got a letter back from her with the words 'Patrick, if you ever had any feelings for me, please do not contact me again,' written on the outside of the envelope. Even though my heart was broken, I had to accept that was what she wanted. I thought perhaps she had met someone else. How I wish she had told me the truth; if I had known what my mother and Tabitha had done, I could have told her it wasn't true. We could have walked away from the lot of them.'

'So what happened then?' Grace asked, hanging on his every word.

He sighed. 'By this stage, the estate's finances were in a dire condition. We were haemorrhaging money every month and had to sell a lot of our artwork and say goodbye to our beloved housekeeper, Mrs Mooney, who had worked with our family for almost fifty years. As I watched her walking down the avenue, a suitcase in each hand, I felt a huge pressure on my shoulders. It was up to me to save them. Generations of Cavendish men had married strategically, so what made me special? Why should I be any different? My parents managed to convince me that marrying Tabitha was the only way to save Cavendish Hall. They persuaded me that Tabitha would understand how to run a house like ours. The more I thought about it, the more I knew they were probably right. Rosa was a free spirit; I knew she would find life in Cavendish Hall smothering. All the rules and etiquette would stifle her. I tried getting in contact with Rosa one more time, and I called over to the cottage when she returned from college, but she refused to see me. I was defeated, so eventually I agreed to marry Tabitha. Things moved quickly then: the engagement notice was published, the date was set, and it was full steam ahead with the wedding plans.'

'So there you were, revelling in your plans while my poor mother was left pregnant and alone!' Grace went on. Even though Patrick had tried to explain himself, it was still hard to summon up any sympathy for him. 'Didn't you ever wonder about your child?'

'I've thought about you every single day, Grace,' he said sadly. 'On the morning of my wedding to Tabitha I found out through Donie that Rosa had gone into labour. There I was on what should have been the happiest day of my life, but instead I was distraught, thinking that I should have been by her side. I heard that evening that you had been born. People were coming up, shaking my hand and congratulating me on my marriage, but all I could think about was that I was now a father. My baby daughter had entered the world.' He paused. 'I don't know if you realise this…' He hesitated. 'I tried to contact you several times over the years, but your mother was still adamant that she wanted nothing to do with me.'

Grace was stunned. 'You tried to get in contact with me?'

'Of course – many, many times. After you were born, I asked your mother if I could meet you, but she refused and warned me not to try and contact her ever again. I thought about going through my solicitor to gain access to you but I knew Rosa would resent me even more if I dragged her into a legal battle so I sent you birthday gifts every year and presents at Christmas, in the hope that maybe one year, she might change her mind and I might hear from you both. On your eighteenth birthday I even sent you a locket that had belonged to my grandmother, but your mother returned all the gifts to me. I had to respect her wishes, but still I hoped that maybe one day you would write back to me. It was painful to know that I had a child out there I didn't know. I wondered what you looked like – whether you had your mother's fair colouring and wild curls or if you were dark-haired, like my side. When I heard Rosa had died, I thought maybe the time had come to try and make contact with you once again. I was mulling it over, deciding what way was best to approach you, and then I saw you that day in the cove and I recognised you instantly.'

'Didn't you ever bump into one another over the years when my mum was home visiting? Inishbeg Cove is a small place.'

'Sometimes I did see Rosa in the street or swimming in the cove with Maggie, but even though I longed to talk to her, I had to respect her wishes. I kept my distance.'

'So what happened between you and Tabitha?' Grace asked. 'Are you still married?'

'God, no.' Patrick shook his head. 'I tried my best to make our marriage work, for Tabitha's sake, but it was doomed before it had even begun. As it turned out, her family didn't have as much money as my parents were led to believe, so money was still tight. Tabitha loved playing lady of the manor, whereas I hated all that kind of thing. She just didn't get how times had changed from my parents' day, and refused to accept that the era of big estate houses being their own economy were over. We couldn't afford the upkeep on the house with the expenditure we had. She didn't understand why we couldn't maintain the lifestyle that my parents had enjoyed, with kitchen staff, butlers and chauffeurs. She wanted the same level of service that we had had generations ago, and when I tried to make changes to save money, she went behind my back and spent it anyway. When the money ran out, Tabitha left me for a tech millionaire. It seemed she hadn't taken me for better or for worse, after all.' A wry smile played at the corners of his lips.

Grace couldn't help being irritated by his parents' assertion that Tabitha was a better match than her mother had been, when in fact it had been Tabitha who hadn't been able to hack life in Cavendish Hall when the money had dried up.

'To be honest, we should never have married,' Patrick continued. 'We were not suited.' He stood up and threw more logs on the fire, sending a spray of embers up into the chimney. 'And so Cavendish Hall fell into rack and ruin anyway.'

Although Grace was still angry with Patrick, talking to him today had helped her to see his side of the story. She had come over here expecting a showdown, but it had turned out so differently. Listening to him tell the sorry tale of his ill-fated love affair with her mother, Grace had learnt that Patrick had his own share of pain: he had missed out on thirty-one years of her life because Rosa wouldn't let him in. He had suffered too.

'Maggie said my mother never got over you,' Grace said in a low voice.

Tears filled his eyes. 'If I could have done things differently, I would, believe me. I often wonder how my life would have turned out if I hadn't wasted time trying to persuade my parents to allow me to marry Rosa. If I'd followed my heart, walked away from this place and started a new life with her, I think I would have been a hell of a lot happier.'

'Did you have any more children?' Grace ventured. She felt a frisson of excitement. To think she could have siblings! She had always wondered what it might be like to have a brother or sister.

Patrick shook his head. 'Sadly not – it's just you. You're the only heir to Cavendish Hall.'

The words hit Grace like a slap. Was that what he thought she was after?

'This isn't what this is about. I didn't come here to lay claim to your estate, if that's what you're thinking!' she blazed. 'This place caused so much pain for my mother.'

'I'm sorry – I didn't mean to be insensitive. It's just that you're my daughter, and I have gifted it to you in my will,' he stated matter-of-factly.

Grace was shocked. 'You've left it to me in your will? Even though up until recently you had never even met me, and if I hadn't come here today, we might never have spoken? I might not even have wanted it!' She couldn't believe he would sign over his estate to a stranger, even if she was his biological daughter.

He shrugged. 'I had to put a succession plan in place in the event of my death. Everything goes to you, to do with as you want. I'm not getting any younger. It needs new blood, somebody creative with energy and enthusiasm. You can take it on and try and make something of it, or sell it. Frankly, I don't care what you do with it. It might seem strange, but I have no attachment to the place any more, other than as a roof over my head, because in my experience this place is just as much a curse as it is a blessing.'

Grace was stunned by his forthrightness – and by the revelation that in the future this place was to be hers. Her head began to spin. It was too much to take in.

'I–I don't know what to say...' was all she could manage.

'I can't tell you how happy I am to finally talk to you after all this time. I have longed to meet you for so many years. I would love the opportunity to get to know you, if you would let me?'

Grace thought about what Patrick had done to her mother. He had made poor decisions and had been overshadowed by his parents, but he had paid a heavy price. His life seemed lonely and full of regrets – and when he had tried to put things right, her mother had thwarted his every advance. Grace knew how stubborn Rosa could be when she made up her mind about something. If she thought Patrick had betrayed her, her mum would never have forgiven him. Something inside Grace wanted to get to know Patrick. She might not like the man she discovered, but she wanted to at least try. If her mother's loss had taught her anything, it was that life was too short to hold grudges. She wanted to give Patrick a chance.

'Let's give it a try,' she said. It was time to move forward and forgive.

14

In the café Penny and Ruairí had just seen off the morning coffee-to-go crowd and were catching their breath before the lunchtime rush.

'So did Tadgh manage to find out anything more about the mysterious Undercover Critic?' Ruairí asked as he wiped down the counter tops. Penny was restocking steaming scones fresh from the oven behind the glass counter. Tadgh had just left with his takeaway coffee, heading up to the restaurant, looking as though he had the weight of the world on his shoulders. Penny could tell by the way he had spent the whole night tossing and turning in bed beside her that he hadn't got a wink of sleep, and she knew that the letter from the HSE was on his mind.

'Well he called the paper. Apparently the review arrived anonymously by email. Even though the editor had never worked with this person before, he decided to publish it anyway to fill up space.'

'A paper never refuses ink,' Ruairí said dryly. 'And I guess Tadgh tried to contact them using the same email address?'

'He did, but he got no response.'

'There's more than a whiff of something strange going on here.'

'Well, the plot thickens, because you'll never guess what's happened since.'

'Go on…'

'He received a letter from the HSE yesterday, claiming that they're investigating a case of food poisoning in the restaurant! He's never had a case of food poisoning in all the years he's been at the helm. They're sending down an environmental health officer to carry out an investigation next week.'

Ruairí scoffed. 'There's more chance of getting bleach poisoning in Tadgh's. It's the cleanest restaurant I know. There's definitely something fishy going on here.'

Penny sighed. 'Tadgh is so down about it all. He's starting to doubt himself – he thinks he's not up to scratch since the accident. I know I'm biased, but he's a great chef and he runs a damn good restaurant.'

'Someone clearly has it in for him. Do you think Joe could be behind it?'

'The thought did cross my mind all right,' Penny admitted, resting her back against the counter top. 'But I don't think he cares enough to go to all that trouble.' Although her ex-husband was moody and self-absorbed, she knew he wasn't vindictive. That wasn't his style, and from what she had heard from her friends in Dublin, he had already moved on with someone new so he probably couldn't care less about Penny and Tadgh. 'He seems happy being left alone to get on with his art and whatever else he gets up to. Joe would have no problem telling me how he feels; if he was angry, I'd know all about it. He wouldn't be underhand about doing things.'

Just then the bell tinkled and a customer entered. Penny recognised him immediately as the man who had been at Tadgh's reopening party. She elbowed Ruairí. 'Enter suspect A.'

Ruairí followed her line of vision and saw the man making his way towards them.

'What can I get you?' Ruairí asked politely.

'I'll have a pot of tea, and that apple tart looks delicious – I'll take a slice of that too, please.'

'If you want to take a seat, I'll bring it down to you.'

As Tadgh filled a teapot with hot water, Penny watched the man. He sat down at the table beside the stove. He opened his backpack and took out the same notebook he had been writing in in the restaurant.

'I'd better not be starring in his next review.' Ruairí grimaced, standing beside her and eyeing him up. 'I'll have to be on my best behaviour.' He loaded a tray with the tea and tart and brought it to the table.

'Here you go, sir.' Ruairí set the teapot and plate on the table.

'Can I get some extra cream for my tart, please?' the man asked. 'I know it's not good for the arteries, but there's nothing nicer than an apple tart with a good dollop of fresh cream.'

'Of course. I'll bring it now.' Ruairí went back behind the counter. 'Let's hope the cream is creamy enough,' he muttered to Penny, filling a small pot with freshly whipped cream before returning to the man's table.

Ruairí noticed that the customer had his notebook open on the table and he peered over his head, trying to read what he was writing, but the letters were too small.

'Hard at work?' He set the pot of cream down on the table.

'Always chasing deadlines,' the man replied.

'Are you a writer?' Ruairí probed.

'I am, for my sins.'

'What is it that you write?'

'Today, nothing.' The man laughed, a mischievous twinkle in his eye. 'I'm trying to write a review, but I seem to have the dreaded writer's block.'

Ruairí left him alone to enjoy his tea and tart. He went back behind the counter and beckoned Penny into the kitchen. 'I think we definitely have our man,' he hissed. 'He told me he's a writer – and he's working on a review. I tried to peek into his notebook but I couldn't make out what he was writing.' He folded his arms across his chest.

'Hmm, well, let's make sure he leaves here happy,' Penny said worriedly. 'The last thing I want is for you to get slated in next week's edition.'

They went back to work, loading the oven with bread and cakes and serving a steady stream of customers. Not long afterwards, Maggie arrived after her swim. Unusually, she was alone.

'Good morning, Maggie,' Penny greeted her. 'Grace isn't with you today?'

'She, er... she had something on...'

Penny noticed Maggie's face took on a faraway look. She seemed to be on edge about something and Penny got the distinct feeling that she wanted to change the subject. 'So how was your swim?' she asked, feeling it was safer territory.

'Great, thanks. You can't beat a dip in the Atlantic on a day like today,' Maggie replied, brightening up again.

Ruairí looked out the drizzle-spattered window at the leaves that were dancing in the wind. 'We'll take your word for it.'

'Oh, I'll convert you one of these days, Ruairí.' Maggie

wagged a finger at him. 'I'll take the usual, please, love.' She looked around the café, then her eyes narrowed. The writer was standing up and packing up his belongings.

'Isn't that the fella that gave Tadgh the nasty review in *The Atlantic Times*?' Maggie whispered.

'We don't know it's him for sure,' Ruairí said. 'But he's a writer and he told me that he's working on a review...'

'If it looks like a duck, walks like a duck and quacks like a duck...' Maggie replied, eyeballing him from across the room. 'The cheek of him! I feel like going over there and giving him a piece of my mind.'

'Take it easy, Maggie,' Penny warned. 'We can't go around accusing him without having proof.' The last thing she wanted was for Maggie to cause a scene; that would be a sure-fire way to have Ruairí's café torn to pieces in his next review.

Maggie stared at him. 'Well, we all know it's him even if he's too cowardly to put his name to his review!'

They watched the man as he put his notebook into his backpack, before slinging it over his shoulder, oblivious to his audience.

'Thanks for that,' he called as he passed them on his way out. 'It was delicious. That pastry!' He pinched his thumb and index finger together and kissed them in the Italian way. 'Amazing!'

Ruairí was about to thank him when Maggie jumped in. 'Let's hope you'll be a bit kinder in your critique this time,' she retorted.

The man looked at her, clearly perplexed. 'Okay ... yes ... well, er, I'd best be off.'

'Maggie!' Ruairí cried as soon as he had left. 'What did you say that for?'

'He'll go to town on poor Ruairí now,' Penny added anxiously.

Maggie tutted. 'Woe betide him! If he starts messing around with this place as well, he'll have me to answer to.'

15

Grace opened the door of the cottage and stepped inside its warmth. A swirl of leaves rushed inside in her wake. The wind had picked up in the time she had been at Cavendish Hall.

'Well?' Maggie asked, hurrying over to her as Grace struggled to close the door against the wind. 'How did it go? I've been worried sick about you. You've been gone for hours.'

'Have I?' Grace asked looking at her watch before fixing her windswept hair.

'I was trying to call you.'

Grace fished her phone out of her pocket, and saw that it was switched off. 'Sorry, I think it's dead.'

'Come on,' Maggie said, walking back to the sofa. She sat down and patted the cushion beside her. 'Sit down and tell me everything.'

Grace followed and flopped down beside her aunt. 'It went well, I think. He was nice.'

'Nice?' Maggie cried bitterly. 'So he acknowledged the fact that he is your father then, did he?'

Grace nodded. 'He couldn't have been more welcoming. He said he had been waiting years for this day to arrive and that he knew as soon as he saw me in the cove that I was his child.'

'It's a pity he couldn't have been as enthusiastic over thirty years ago!' Maggie retorted.

'They deceived him, Maggie.'

Maggie narrowed her eyes. 'Who did?'

'His mother and Tabitha. He never knew that they had called over to my mum. So when he received her letter with no explanation telling him to get lost and never to come near her again, he couldn't understand what had changed between them. He tried to talk to her but she refused to listen to him.' Grace filled Maggie in on Patrick's side of the story.

'But that still doesn't explain why he didn't tell Rosa that he was already in a relationship with Tabitha.'

'That's the thing,' Grace explained, 'he *wasn't* with Tabitha at that stage. She and Mrs Cavendish lied. They fabricated the whole thing to break Patrick and Mum up.'

'Well Patrick and Tabitha announced their engagement just a few weeks later, so there must have been something going on between them,' Maggie snapped.

'Patrick told me that his parents had been putting pressure on him to marry Tabitha for a long time even before he met Mum; they believed the match would be financially advantageous for them. The Cavendish family were having money troubles back then and they hoped they would see some money directed their way. Tabitha was very keen on him, apparently, but Patrick had no interest in her. After Mum found out she was pregnant and he told them that he wanted to marry her, his parents wouldn't entertain the idea, so it seems that Mrs Cavendish and Tabitha hatched the plan to visit Mum and tell her that Tabitha was already in a relationship with Patrick. They schemed the whole thing up together. Patrick never knew a thing about it – he was shocked when I told him.'

'So he wasn't two-timing your mother?' Maggie asked cautiously.

'He said Mum was the only woman he has ever loved.'

'So why did he get married to Tabitha so soon after he and Rosa broke up?'

Grace could see that Maggie's head was in a whirl as she tried to process this version of events. 'According to Patrick, he was heartbroken when he got Mum's letter ending things between them. He tried to talk to her to find out what was going on, but she wouldn't listen to what he had to say. In the meantime his parents were putting pressure on him to marry Tabitha to save the estate. It sounds as though he was so defeated by it all that he just gave in to his parents' wishes in the end.'

Maggie shook her head. 'He could have walked away from them, y'know, if he loved your mother enough. Why was he waiting around for his parents' approval?'

'It seems he really believed he could get them to change their mind. It's his biggest regret,' Grace said sadly.

'And it still doesn't excuse the fact that he knew he had a child,' Maggie went on. 'He knew Rosa was pregnant when things ended between them!'

'I know, Maggie, but he told me that he tried to keep in contact with me but Mum would never allow it. After I was born, he called here but she told him never to darken her door again. Apparently he wrote to me on my birthday and at Christmas every year, but Mum always returned his letters and gifts unopened. Did she ever mention that to you?'

'No, she didn't, but do you blame her?' Maggie said defensively. 'After what he did to her?'

'No, of course not. After everything that happened to her back then, I know she made the choices that she thought were for the best, but I feel sad for what might have been. I spent so many years wondering who my father was when I could have had him in my life if things had been different.'

'Your mother did the best she could,' Maggie said. 'She was both mother and father to you growing up. I don't think it's fair on her memory to have some stranger waltz in and play happy families, now that the hard work is done.'

'I know, Maggie. I'm not having a go at her decision to cut him out of her life without giving him a chance to explain himself. Who knows? I might have done the same thing myself if I was in her situation. I guess there are so many "what ifs" to think about,' Grace said. 'What might have happened if Mrs Cavendish and Tabitha hadn't done what they did? Or what if Patrick had stood up to his parents and told him that he was marrying Mum with or without their blessing? What might life have been like if I had known Patrick was my father when I was a child? We'll never know.' Grace paused, knowing what she was about to tell Maggie next would come as a bombshell. She still hadn't even got her own head around it yet. 'There's something else…' she began.

Maggie eyed her warily. 'What is it?'

'He's left Cavendish Hall to me in his will.'

Maggie's mouth fell open. 'Cavendish Hall – to you?'

'He has named me as his sole heir.'

'But why on earth would he do that? Sure, he had never even met you until a few weeks ago!' Laughter bubbled up inside Maggie at the notion of her niece swanning around

Cavendish Hall as lady of the manor. The whole thing was preposterous.

'What? What's so funny?' Grace asked, feeling confused. She hadn't expected Maggie to react like this.

'It's crazy!' Maggie spluttered.

'I know – it's mad, isn't? But he wants me to have it.'

The lines between Maggie's brow knitted together in a V. 'Do you believe him?'

'Well, that's what he said.' Grace suddenly began to doubt herself. As she told Maggie what Patrick had told her, it did sound ludicrous. 'I know it's a huge shock. He said I can either sell it or try and make something of it. He doesn't seem to care. His heart isn't in it any more. I think inheriting the estate and following his parents' wishes has been a burden on Patrick for his whole life, and he just wants rid of it now.'

'I don't trust that fella.' Maggie shook her head.

'Oh, you should see it, Maggie!' Grace said, trying to hide the excitement that was creeping into her voice as she thought about Cavendish Hall's magnificence, but failing miserably. 'Even though the wallpaper is peeling off the walls and the house is bloody freezing, it's so beautiful. It's in such a pitiful state, though; it needs someone to take it on and give it a lot of TLC. But I don't know anything about old houses, and even if I did, I don't have the money to restore something like that.'

'The place sounds like a money pit. Don't get ahead of yourself.' Maggie tapped her index finger to her temple. 'Patrick might not even be all there, Gracie. You don't have to take it on if you don't want to, love – you don't owe Patrick anything.'

'I know, Maggie. I don't know what to do, to be honest. I

finally get to meet my father and then I get this news too … my head is spinning.'

Maggie put an arm around Grace's shoulder and pulled her close. 'You've had a big day today. It's a lot to take in. I know you're excited, but I don't want you to get hurt. Just take it easy, love; you don't have to rush into anything.'

'You're right,' Grace said, feeling reality slam into her. Just hours ago, she hadn't known her father, and now she had met him and learnt the truth about his ill-fated love story with her mother, then the news about her inheritance of Cavendish Hall had landed on her doorstep. Maggie was right. She hardly knew Patrick, he had already let her mother down, and she needed to be careful that he didn't do the same thing to her too.

16

The sky above was alight with streaks of indigo, salmon pink and neon orange as the sun rose on a new day. Maggie was too early for the swimmers that morning, but she hadn't been able to sleep. She knew a swim was the only thing that would help after a night spent tossing and turning, so she pulled back the duvet, got up and got ready to go down to the cove.

She had been sleeping badly ever since Grace had met Patrick. Maggie was anxious about it all. She knew Grace was thrilled to have finally met her father, but then he had dropped the bombshell that she would be the one to inherit Cavendish Hall. No matter what had gone on before with Patrick and Rosa, Maggie needed to remember that Grace had only just discovered who her father was, and it was natural for her to be excited to find out more about the man and the estate that would all be hers one day ... but still, she was uneasy. She was suspicious of Patrick and his intentions. Was he filling her niece full of empty promises to help reel her in? Was he so lonely sitting up there in that big house of his that he was trying to lure Grace into his life, now that he knew her mother was no longer around to protect her? Maggie felt a pressure to protect her niece; it had been Rosa's dying wish for Maggie to keep an eye on her daughter when she was no longer around. She really hoped that Patrick wasn't making a fool of Grace, like he had done to Rosa all those years ago. Patrick had told Grace a different version of events but even still, there was no escaping the fact that Rosa's life had been destroyed because Patrick hadn't had the backbone to stand up to his parents all those years ago.

Maggie couldn't help being awestruck as the sun rose higher, gilding the sky with a bright light that spread like a veil across the headland. It had been a long time since she had taken the time to watch the sunrise. Even on the rare occasions when she was awake at that hour of the morning, if she had been catching an early flight, for example, she was usually too sleepy to pay attention to it. She remembered the long nights she had spent at Rosa's bedside as her sister had neared her final days. Maggie had watched many sunrises with her sister's frail hand cradled inside her own but she had been too tired to appreciate them. There was something about being in nature that helped her heart be at peace. She found her eyes begin to fill with tears from the sheer beauty of it all.

She waded through the shallow water. The tide was out, so she had to go out quite far to submerge herself. The hard ripples of the sea bed pressed into the soles of her booties as she walked, then suddenly the sea floor dropped away beneath her feet like a step and she was plunged into the icy Atlantic water. Pain shot through her ankle. Water rushed over her face. She gulped and gasped as she tried to get her balance, but pain seared through her and she was upended once more. She tumbled through the water until she had lost her bearings. It was as though she was being spun inside a washing machine: she couldn't see, she couldn't breathe. She tried to scream as she was tossed and turned, but salty water rushed in and filled her mouth and lungs, and her chest began to burn. Eventually she saw a flash of sky. She tried once more to stand up but the water won, pulling her under again before she could manage to take a breath. As her body grew weaker in its battle against the ocean, she could feel herself slipping away – she didn't have the energy left to fight. *This is it for me,* she thought as the sea tossed her around. *This is the end. This is how I'm going to go.*

Suddenly she felt something around her chest, pulling her from behind, and she realised with a wave of relief that someone was holding her up. Her head finally emerged from the water and she saw the pale-yellow sky above her. She gasped for air, coughing up water and spluttering. A pair of strong arms picked her up and carried her through the water. When they reached the shore, the man laid her down on the sand. It was only when she got to see his face that she realised it was the man from the café – the Undercover Critic. His features were creased with worry as he tried to turn her into the recovery position, but she cried out from the pain in her ankle.

'Did you hurt your foot?' he asked.

She could only nod, unable to form the words to respond, coughing up more salty water. Pain shot through her ankle as she retched onto the sand. She was cold, right down to the marrow of her bones, and she couldn't stop shaking. Seeming to notice her chattering teeth, he ran over to where he had left his coat on the sand and hurried back with it. He placed it over her like a blanket, but it offered little in the way of warmth. As she shivered on the damp sand, her eyes felt heavy, and began to close.

'I think I'd better call an ambulance,' she heard him say as he took his phone out of his rucksack. She was so weary. She closed her eyes and began to drift off, but he kept talking to her and wouldn't just let her sleep.

Maggie didn't know how much time had passed. When she opened her eyes again, she saw blue lights circling above them in the cove. Had it been hours or minutes? She had lost all sense of time. Moments later, the ambulance crew ran across the sand towards them.

As they transferred her to a stretcher, she shouted out as pain shot through her foot.

'We'll have some pain relief for you in the ambulance, lovey,' one of the female paramedics said.

'Can I go with her?' she heard the man ask.

'Of course,' another voice said. 'Jump in.'

And despite everything he had done, she was so glad to have him there by her side.

~

When Maggie woke up, the first thing she saw was the concerned face of the Undercover Critic. It felt like she was looking at him through the spy-glass in a door. Every part of her seemed to hurt. She shut her eyes once more.

'Are you okay, Maggie?' he asked.

She opened her eyes again. This time she could focus better. She looked around the unfamiliar room. 'Where am I?' she asked.

'You're in hospital. You gave me quite the fright.'

Horrible flashbacks of tumbling through the water, gasping for air that wouldn't come, filled her head. 'Wh-what happened?'

'I was out for an early morning walk and saw you. I thought perhaps you were just swimming, but after a moment I realised you were in trouble so I ran in after you.'

'My ankle…' Maggie said, as it all came rushing back to her.

'They've X-rayed it. It's not broken, thankfully, but it's badly sprained,' he said. 'They didn't want to tell me anything because I'm not family but I managed to squeeze an update out of a very nice nurse.'

Suddenly she remembered Grace: she was probably worried sick, waking up and realising that Maggie wasn't at home. 'Grace – I need to tell my niece where I am–'

'She's already here. She just nipped down to get a coffee a few minutes ago. She'll be back soon.'

'But how did she…' – Maggie paused to catch a breath – 'know what happened?'

'I'd seen you chatting with Ruairí in the café so I knew you were friendly with him. I phoned the café from the hospital and told him what had happened, and he called up to the cottage to tell Grace and bring her to the hospital. She got a fright, but she's okay.'

Maggie felt a swell of gratitude to this man – not just for saving her life, but for his forethought in calling Ruairí so he could give the news to Grace. Hot tears filled Maggie's eyes as she realised how close she had come to drowning. He had saved her life. She thanked her lucky stars that he had been on the beach that morning. Otherwise – well, she didn't want to think about that…

'Thank you,' she whispered, then realised she didn't even know his name. 'Sorry, I don't even know you—'

'I'm Liam. Liam Manley.'

'Well, Liam, I owe my life to you. Thank you.'

'How are you feeling now?' Liam asked, his face creased in concern.

'I'm okay.' Her chest felt as though there was a tonne of concrete blocks piled on top of her ribs and her throat was raw, but none of that mattered. She was alive and that in itself was miraculous. 'When I went over on my ankle, I just couldn't get up again. I thought I was going to die,' Maggie admitted. 'Thank God you were there, Liam, or it could have ended very differently.' A shiver snaked through her at how close she had come to facing her own mortality. The cards of life had dealt her a second hand today.

'We both got a fright, Maggie. It just shows that, no matter how well you know the sea, it can still turn on you when you least expect it.'

Just then, she saw Grace's concerned face appear round the door. She rushed over to Maggie's bedside when she saw that she was awake. 'Oh thank God, you're okay, Auntie Maggie!' She dissolved into tears.

'I'm sorry, Gracie.' Maggie was contrite. What must have been going through her niece's head? Grace had just lost her mother. Maggie was all she had left. She was mortified by her silly mishap. Trust her to turn what should have been a quick dip in the ocean into a calamity. 'I'm a clumsy old fool!'

'Will you stop apologising, you crazy woman?' Grace laughed through her tears.

Maggie sighed and fell back against the pillows. 'When can I get out of this place? I feel like a big eejit.'

'Take it easy, Maggie,' Liam advised. 'The doctor said

they need to keep an eye on your vital signs for a few hours in case of secondary drowning.'

Maggie looked at her niece, then at Liam. He might have written a bad review about Tadgh's restaurant, but that didn't take away from the fact that she had got a second chance because of him. She owed him her life.

17

Under a steel-grey sky, Tadgh made his way up the headland along the path that led to his restaurant the next day. He had just rounded a rock that jutted out of the cliff face when he saw a group of men in neon yellow hi-vis jackets working ahead on the path. He picked up his pace, curious about what was going on. He didn't recall receiving any notice about works taking place. As he got closer, he saw they were shovelling a pile of rubble that was blocking the way.

'What's going on here?' he called out across the tape they had erected to cordon off the path. He waited while one of the men put down his shovel and walked over to meet him.

'We've had to close the path,' he said when he reached Tadgh.

'But why?'

'Council orders. There was a small landslide. It's too dangerous to let people walk along the path now; we have no choice but to close it.'

'But I walked home along here last night, and it was fine then.'

The man shrugged. 'It must have happened during the night. We had a call from a concerned member of the public about it this morning.'

Tadgh couldn't imagine that many other people had been down this path between last night and this morning. The landslide could only have been discovered by someone who was out for a very early walk – and walkers didn't usually bother coming down here, because the path ended at the restaurant.

'But my restaurant is down there.' He pointed towards the arched doorway in the distance that led inside the cave.

'I'm sorry, but by order of the council we can't let you through. It's too hazardous.'

'Okay, so when will it be cleared?' Tadgh looked at his watch, mentally calculating how long he had to get ready for that evening's service.

'The team and I are clearing it, but we can't let anybody use it until we've had an engineer assess the cliff face.'

'And when might that be?' Tadgh asked, trying to keep impatience out of his voice.

'Probably middle to late next week.'

'Middle to late next week!' Tadgh repeated. 'But I've customers booked in for dinner tonight!'

'Unfortunately, you won't be in a position to reopen until the engineer gives you the all clear.'

Dread flooded Tadgh. What if the engineer deemed the path structurally unsound? He had always known that his restaurant, which was built into a cave in the cliff face, was at the mercy of coastal erosion, but he had never known any issues with the cliff or the path in all the time he had worked there, and neither had his parents before him. The location certainly came with its challenges but the worst thing that had ever happened was not being able to open in stormy weather because the path became too hazardous.

'Phil, come on – we need to get a move on here,' another man called over to him.

'That's the boss,' the man said. 'I'd better get back to work.'

'So that's it?' Tadgh called after him, frustration boiling up inside him. 'I can't get into my own restaurant?' He wanted to pull down the tape, climb over the pile of rubble and storm up the path, regardless of what the man was saying.

'I'm sorry, sir, but we don't make the rules. The engineer will let you know the outcome once they've had a chance to assess it.' The man turned around, picked up his shovel and went back to work, leaving Tadgh with no choice but to head back to the village.

∼

'WHAT ARE YOU DOING BACK HERE?' Penny asked as the bell over the café door tinkled and she saw Tadgh enter once again. She had only seen him off with his coffee-to-go half an hour ago. His face was clouded over, and she could tell something was wrong.

'The council have closed the cliff path!'

Her jaw dropped. 'What? Why would they do that?'

'There was a small landslide from the cliff above. They said that they received a call about it this morning. I walked home along it last night and it was fine,' he said with more than a hint of bitterness. 'It'll be next week before a council engineer gets out to assess it, and in the meantime I can't open my restaurant.'

'Oh, Tadgh, I'm sorry.'

'First it was the review of the reopening night, then the letter from the HSE about the food poisoning, and now this... It seems to be one thing after another lately.'

'You can't seem to catch a break at all,' Penny agreed. Was it more than just coincidence that these events were happening at the same time? she wondered. The feeling that there was something more behind it all was strengthening.

Just then the bell over the door tinkled again, and Liam entered. Liam had startled Ruairí and Penny in the café the day before with his phone call from the hospital telling them about Maggie. Not having Grace's mobile number, Ruairí had left Penny to hold the fort while he had driven up to Maggie's cottage, broken the news to Grace, and taken her straight to the hospital. Penny had told Tadgh all about the drama when he had come in from the restaurant the night before.

'Ah, if it isn't the hero himself!' Ruairí announced, coming out of the kitchen and joining Penny and Tadgh at the counter. 'Tell me, Liam, how is Maggie doing?'

'I phoned Grace earlier. She's recovering well at home.'

'That's a relief,' Tadgh said.

'That's why I'm here, actually. I want to call on her to see how she is. Tell me, what does she like to eat?' he asked.

'Lemon drizzle cake,' Penny and Ruairí answered together.

'Well, that settles it.' Liam chuckled. 'Could you box me up a loaf of that, please?'

'Absolutely.' Ruairí lifted the cake into a box and tied it with a red ribbon.

Liam opened his wallet to pay, but Ruairí told him the cake was on the house.

'Thank you, Ruairí, that's very kind of you. Now tell me, whereabouts does she live?'

Ruairí gave him directions to Maggie's coastguard cottage. As Penny watched him leave, she found it difficult to believe that the man who had saved Maggie's life was the same man who seemed hell-bent on destroying Tadgh's restaurant. 'It's hard to think that he might be the Undercover Critic,' Penny began after a moment. 'He seems too... well... *nice*.'

'I have to agree with you,' Ruairí admitted. 'When he phoned me yesterday from the hospital to tell me what had happened, he couldn't have been more concerned. He doesn't seem to have a nasty bone in his body.'

'Do you think we've got it wrong then?' Tadgh asked.

'Well, he did tell me he was a writer...' Ruairí said, his voice laced with uncertainty. 'And he had his notebook out at your party.'

'And he told you that he was working on a review that day in the café,' Penny added.

'Oh, who knows?' Tadgh threw his hands in the air in frustration. 'I don't think I'll ever get to the bottom of it all.'

18

Grace set Maggie up on the sofa beside the fire and placed a rug over her knees for extra warmth. She had just thrown a piece of turf into the hearth and was bent over stoking the flames when there was a knock at the cottage door. Maggie pulled back the blanket, reached for her crutches and made to get up.

'Don't you dare move, Maggie O'Neill,' Grace warned, putting the poker down and going over to answer the door.

'I could get used to this,' Maggie said, pulling the rug around her and leaning back against the sofa cushions. She was exhausted after her near-death experience the day before. She still had the remains of a cough as her lungs tried to recover, and every breath felt as though her chest was being stabbed by a million tiny daggers, but she was feeling a lot better.

Grace opened the door and Maggie turned to see Liam standing there, holding a small box.

'Hello, Grace, hello, Maggie,' he said.

'Come on in.' Grace gestured.

'I hope I'm not intruding. I just wanted to see how you were doing, Maggie.' Liam stepped into the cottage.

'I'm still here, anyway. You can't keep a good thing down,' she said with a wink.

'I ... er ... brought you this.' Nervously, he handed her the box he was carrying. 'Ruairí mentioned that you're partial to a slice of his lemon drizzle cake,' he added sheepishly.

'Guilty as charged. I hope Ruairí didn't reveal any more of my deep, dark secrets.' Maggie laughed. 'That's so kind of you – thanks, Liam. Not only did you save my life, but you come bearing cake. You're some man for one man!'

'Why don't I make us all a pot of tea to go with it?' Grace suggested.

'Take a seat,' Maggie ordered Liam, while Grace began filling the kettle. Liam removed his coat and gloves and warmed his hands over the flames of the turf fire for a moment before sitting in the armchair.

'Thanks again for what you did yesterday. I can't imagine what it was like for you, going for a lovely sunrise stroll along the cove to be greeted by the sight of me being thrown around like that,' Maggie said self-deprecatingly.

'I'm just glad I was there, Maggie,' Liam said modestly.

'Well, I'm going to call you Mitch Buchannon from now on,' Maggie replied.

Liam chortled. 'I do have a look of David Hasselhoff all right.' He paused and looked her up and down. 'You're looking good, all things considered.'

'I do tend to look a bit better with my clothes on,' Maggie joked, then cringed as soon as the words had left her mouth. *What was she thinking?* 'I mean ... obviously, I wasn't swimming naked or anything,' she added quickly, feeling the heat radiating from her cheeks all the way up to the tips of her ears. 'Oh God.' She was mortified. Then laughter bubbled up inside her; she couldn't help it. It frothed up and spilled from her lips and turned into real, belly-aching giggles.

'I know what you meant.' Liam laughed along with her.

Tears were pouring down their faces as Grace set the teapot down on the coffee table. 'What's so funny?' she asked, looking at them in amusement.

'Th-the clothes!' Maggie spluttered, trying to explain but unable to get the words out without convulsing into laughter again. Grace turned to Liam for an explanation, but he was in no better state than Maggie.

Grace shook her head at the pair of them. 'Honestly, you're like a pair of bold children,' she joked as she began slicing the cake.

'So, as well as doing a bit of lifeguarding, what brings you to Inishbeg Cove?' Maggie asked when she had finally recovered. She wanted to know more about this mysterious man and where he had come from.

'My wife's parents were from the area. We use their old cottage as a holiday home.'

'So whereabouts is your cottage?' Maggie asked, making an appreciative sound as she took a bite of the fluffy lemon drizzle cake, the tangy flavour crumbling in her mouth.

'Further up the headland on the Top Road. Sea Spray Cottage is its name. It's a small white house covered in wisteria with a turquoise front door.'

'Oh, I know the one,' Maggie said. 'It always has an explosion of roses and hydrangeas along the fence in the summertime.'

'That's the one,' he said, swallowing a mouthful of cake. 'Ingrid's grandmother was a great gardener. She planted all those flowers and they still bloom every summer. Her family were the O'Donnells, but they're all dead now.'

'Ah, I remember old Mr and Mrs O'Donnell from when I was a child. They had a maroon Cortina if I recall rightly, but that was a long time ago now.'

'Ingrid would have been their granddaughter. Her father moved to Dublin in the fifties to study, and he met Ingrid's mother there. He was an only child so he got the cottage after old Mr and Mrs O'Donnell passed on. Ingrid's parents used it as a holiday home, then they left it to Ingrid and me when they died. We used to come down here for a couple of weeks every summer when the boys were small, and sometimes for Easter or mid-term break too, but they're grown up now and have their own lives. We've had some great times here over the years,' he said nostalgically.

'So you've been holidaying here for all these years? Imagine – I've never once seen you.'

He took a sip of his tea. 'These days I don't get down as often as I would like...' He trailed off and Maggie was sure she saw a something in his eyes that told her there was more to this story.

'So, how long are you staying this time? Is it just a short break?' Maggie asked.

'I haven't really decided. I'm trying to come up with ideas. I seem to be suffering from a touch of writer's block. I hoped that the scenery down here might inspire something, but nothing is coming.' Liam groaned.

'What do you write?' Grace asked, intrigued.

'Crime thrillers. I write under the pen name of Thomas Morgan.'

'Are you the one who writes the Detective Roche series?' Grace asked.

Liam nodded.

'My Mum loved those books,' she said sadly. 'They helped pass the time when she was in the hospital getting her chemo.'

'I'm glad to hear that they helped in some small way,' Liam said kindly.

'Is that why you're always scribbling in that notebook?' Maggie asked.

'Well sometimes lines of dialogue or a nice description will come to me out of nowhere and I jot them down because I know I'll forget them if I don't. I have a head like a sieve these days.' He sounded sheepish.

'And what about the review you were writing in the café that day?' Maggie enquired.

Liam looked pensive as he tried to recall what Maggie was referring to. 'Oh, that. It was a review of a debut thriller that the *Irish Times* had asked me to read. Why?'

Maggie looked in his clear green eyes, and knew there was no malice in them. She had only seen kindness from this man since he had saved her life the day before. He certainly wasn't the baddie she had believed he was. 'Oh, Liam, I'm a silly old fool.' She cringed, thinking about how rude she had been to him in the café that day. 'I think I owe you an apology.'

'Whatever for?' He looked taken aback.

'You're not the Undercover Critic, are you?' Maggie asked.

'The Undercover Critic?' Liam shook his head in confusion. 'Who's that?'

Grace explained everything for him.

'And you thought I was the person who wrote the review slating Tadgh?' He looked aghast.

'I'm sorry,' Maggie said, shaking her head. 'I got the wrong end of the stick. It's just that I saw you writing in that little notebook of yours at Tadgh's reopening night, then the review came out, then I saw you again in the café a few days later. Then you told Ruairí that you were a writer and he said you were writing a review... I'm afraid we put two and two together and came up with twenty-two...' Maggie was horrified. How had she ever thought he was responsible for such malicious carry-on? Liam was a decent, honest man, and she felt awful for pinning him as the spiteful person behind Tadgh's bad reviews.

'Don't mention it,' Liam said.

'But if Liam isn't the Undercover Critic, then who is it?' Grace was puzzled.

'I'm not sure. I feel like we're still no closer to solving it.' Maggie sighed heavily.

'I'll have to use it as a juicy plot line for my next book.'

'Well, if all this drama doesn't give you some ideas for a story, then I don't know what will! You should join us for a swim some morning – that'll clear any cobwebs from your head,' Maggie said.

'I think I'll stick to my walks. I still haven't defrosted after my taster session yesterday,' he teased.

'I'm sorry.' Maggie laughed. 'That was different – you had to jump in fully clothed and lug my big arse out of there. I promise you it's not usually that bad. I'm obviously out of action for the next while, but the others will be there if you want to give sea-swimming a try. They meet at eleven every morning. They're all very friendly. I've managed to convert Grace here over the last few weeks – isn't that right?'

'I had no choice. She doesn't take no for answer.' Grace raised her palms to Maggie, as though she was a hostage.

They all laughed and chatted and when Liam was finished his tea and cake, he stood up and folded his coat over his arm. 'Well anyway, I'd best be off.' He pulled his hat down over his ears. 'This book won't write itself.'

'Thanks again, Liam, for everything. I don't think I can ever repay you for what you did yesterday,' Maggie said as he made his way to the door.

'And don't forget, he brought cake too,' Grace added.

'Almost as important as saving my life.' Maggie smiled. 'Maybe we might see you down at the cove for a swim soon?'

'Yes, maybe, I might see you there one of the days.' Liam sounded non-committal. 'Goodbye, ladies.' He stepped out of the cottage and was enveloped by the early evening dusk.

19

A week later Penny collected Lucy from her parents' house after work. As they walked the short distance to Tadgh's, her daughter sang 'Jingle Bells' on repeat the whole way. The class had been learning it in playschool and it was her new favourite song.

'Tadgh?' Penny called as she opened the door and let them into the house.

'I'm in the kitchen,' he replied.

They made their way down the hall and found Tadgh sitting glumly at the table, his phone in his hand. She hated seeing him like this when he should be in his kitchen preparing for that evening's service. Now that he was finally fit again after his accident, she knew it was a kick in the teeth not to be able to go to work. She bent and gave him a kiss on the cheek.

'Hilo, Tadgh,' Lucy sang, running into his arms and climbing onto his knee. Penny's heart swelled seeing how much her daughter adored Tadgh.

'Hi, Lucy.' Tadgh plastered a smile on his face, for Lucy's sake. 'How was playschool?'

'Me learn a new song. I sing it for you.' She wriggled out of Tadgh's arms and jumped down onto the floor.

'This is the forty-seventh time I've heard it,' Penny muttered as Lucy began to sing: 'Gingle bells, gingle bells, gingle alllll the waaaay...'

They clapped when she had finished.

'Bravo!' Tadgh cheered. '"Gingle Bells" is my favourite Christmas song. Take a bow, Ms Lucy.'

Penny noticed how Lucy's little chest puffed out with pride as she grinned at them.

'Now, will you take off your coat and put your school bag down in your room like a good girl?' Penny asked. 'So, how are you doing?' She put an arm around Tadgh's shoulder as Lucy skipped off down the hall.

'I've just called all my customers for the coming week and cancelled their bookings. I couldn't even offer to rebook them for another night because I've no idea when I'll be allowed to open again. Some people were really annoyed – they had made these bookings months ago – and who can blame them?' He shook his head in frustration. 'This is supposed to be my busiest time of the year, but instead I'm staring at an empty reservations book for December. The longer this goes on, the more damage it's going to cause to my business.'

'Oh, Tadgh,' she said, taking a seat beside him at the table. She knew the last thing he wanted to do was let his customers down, but he had no choice.

'I'm just fed up.' His voice was leaden with frustration. 'I need to get back to my restaurant.'

'Did the council have any update for you?' Penny asked. Tadgh had tried calling them every day since they had closed the path, but nobody was ever able to tell him when he might be allowed to reopen.

'I called them again. They said that the engineer has carried out the assessment so at least it's a start, but he's still working on the report.' He groaned. 'The environmental health officer is coming to do their inspection in four days! I need to check that everything is in order and that my records are up to date. Even if the engineer's report arrives before then, and assuming I'm allowed to open up again, I won't have any time to prepare when I can't even get inside the restaurant.'

'Do you think you should cancel the inspector?' Penny suggested. 'I know you just want to get it over with and get back open again, but they won't be impressed if they drive all the way down to Inishbeg Cove and they can't even get into the restaurant.'

'I don't know what to do. I'm still hoping that if the report arrives soon and they deem the path safe, I can go ahead. I'm worried that if I cancel, I might be waiting weeks to get another inspection especially in the run-up to Christmas and they'll think I'm not prepared or, worse still, that I'm trying to hide something. It might raise even more red flags for them, then they'll really go to town on me.'

'Oh, Tadgh, it's cutting it fine. Everything hinges on this engineer's report arriving soon, doesn't it? Did they give you any idea when you can expect to have it?'

He shook his head. 'Nobody will tell me anything. I just have to wait, apparently.' He sighed in exasperation. 'It's all that bloody Undercover Critic's fault!'

'Well, I have news on that front too,' Penny said. 'Grace called into the café earlier. Maggie is doing much better, thankfully, but she said that Liam – that's the man who saved Maggie – is definitely not the Undercover Critic. Apparently he's an author – he told them he carries his notebook around with him to jot down ideas. He was working on a book review that day when Ruairí was chatting to him in the café. We've got the wrong man.'

Tadgh groaned. 'He's an author? What's his name?'

'Liam Manley, but he writes under the name of Thomas Morgan.'

Tadgh was shocked. 'I've read some of his books. Doesn't he write the Detective Roche series?'

Penny nodded. 'That's him – they're good, actually.'

'I feel terrible now for pinning everything on him,' Tadgh said.

'So now we've ruled him out, we're still in the dark about who the hell is doing this to you.' Penny sighed.

Tadgh shook his head. 'It feels like we're going around in circles. Time is running out. I don't know how much longer I can keep going with all this loss of business.'

And it wasn't just the restaurant. Penny was worried about the toll this additional stress was taking on Tadgh so soon after his accident. His restaurant was more than just a business to him; he loved his work and took pride in serving the freshest of local ingredients to his customers. He also had an emotional connection to the place; he felt he owed it to his parents' memory to make it a success. It would kill him to see the business that his grandparents had founded go under. He had worked so hard to learn the ropes as a teenager – not just in the kitchen, but he had taught himself how to own and manage a busy restaurant too. Penny knew he had sacrificed so much over the years to make his restaurant one of the west of Ireland's best-kept secrets; he worked long hours and rarely took holidays. And it wasn't just his livelihood that was at stake; lots of smaller farmers in the environs of the village sold their produce to Tadgh and depended on him for their income. The knock-on impact for all of them if the restaurant were to close would be catastrophic. Tadgh was feeling pressure from all sides to sort this out. They had to get to the bottom of it all – fast.

20

Four days later, Penny and Ruairí were busy working in the café. The scent of cinnamon and ginger sweetened the air from the fresh batch of gingerbread men they had just made. Christmas music was playing on the radio, but although Penny was looking forward to spending her first Christmas with Tadgh since they had rekindled their love, she couldn't seem to get into the spirit of it, no matter how jingly the songs on the radio were. Her head was too consumed with worry for him. His inspection by the environmental health officer was due to take place that afternoon at three o'clock, but she had called him an hour ago and there was still no sign of the council engineer's report. He had decided to give it another hour and if it hadn't arrived by then, he would have no choice but to cancel the inspection. It was down to the wire. Her stomach was knotted with worry as she prayed the report would arrive in time and allow him back into his restaurant today.

Suddenly the door banged open and Tadgh rushed inside.

'What is it?' Penny asked, putting down the jug she was using to froth milk. 'What's wrong?' He was clutching a letter. 'Is it the report?' she asked quickly.

'It just arrived a few minutes ago...' he said breathlessly.

Her stomach somersaulted. 'Go on – what does it say?'

'Don't keep us in suspense,' Ruairí said, draping the tea towel he was carrying over his shoulder and hurrying over to join them.

'There's a load of technical stuff but this is the main bit —' Tadgh held up the letter and began to read out loud. 'From my examination of the cliff face, there is no evidence of either a subsidence or a landslide event. In fact, the rock type found in the rubble doesn't match the cliff stone, and would almost appear to have been deliberately planted there.'

'Oh my God! So they think somebody did it on purpose?' Penny was aghast.

Tadgh nodded. 'It certainly seems like that. It's the only plausible explanation. Somebody must have dumped a load of stone to block the path, then called the council to report a landslide,' Tadgh said bitterly.

'The Undercover Critic strikes again!' Ruairí said, frowning. 'I can't believe someone is going to all this trouble. Why? What's their aim?'

'I don't know what I've done or who I've crossed, but someone has it in for me. I was blaming myself, but now I know I'm not imagining it. It appears that someone is trying to close down my restaurant.'

'But why would anybody want to do that, and why are they going to such great lengths?' Penny was horrified. 'I don't understand it at all.' She shook her head.

'Who knows what their motive is? It could be a disgruntled customer or something more sinister, but either way we have to find out who is doing this and put a stop to them,' Ruairí said.

'But how?' Tadgh asked. 'They've covered their tracks at every turn.'

'Well, now we know that the landslide was staged, let's start by calling the council to see if they can tell us who made the complaint in the first place,' Ruairí suggested.

'I tried that on my way over here, but—' He raised his fingers to make invisible air quotes. 'They aren't at liberty to disclose confidential information.' Tadgh sighed heavily. 'It's one thing to write a nasty review, but to deliberately fake a landslide too is just malicious.'

'And don't forget the alleged food poisoning,' Penny added grimly. 'No doubt they're behind that too.'

'You have to fight back,' Ruairí said.

'But how can I do that when I don't even know who I'm fighting against? I'm worried that the damage has already been done, no matter what the engineer's report says. It's going to be very hard to convince people that the path is safe.'

'Anyone who knows you, knows what a great restaurant you run. We'll help you solve this, we'll get to the bottom of it,' Ruairí promised.

Tadgh glanced as his watch. 'Look, I'd better head on. I've got three hours before this inspector is due to arrive and I've so much to do before then.' He gave Penny a swift kiss on the cheek before dashing out the door.

'I feel awful for him,' Penny said after he had left. 'This is probably the most important visit in his whole time as a restaurateur and he hasn't been able to prepare properly. I just wish there was something I could do.'

'He has nothing to hide – the inspector will surely see what we all see,' Ruairí assured her.

'I hope you're right,' Penny said nervously. She headed into the kitchen and began kneading dough to make a fresh batch of scones. She was plying it with her fingertips and knuckles as she tried hard to concentrate on the task at hand, but her mind kept wandering back to Tadgh and his inspection. Everything hinged on it going well. She didn't like to let her head go there, but Tadgh might not be happy with the outcome of the inspection that day. If the inspector found anything out of line, Tadgh could be served with a closure order – and all because someone wanted his business to fail. He was a pawn in somebody's game – but they didn't know who the game master was. And besides, this wasn't a game to Tadgh; this was his livelihood.

A few minutes later Ruairí entered the kitchen. 'Penny, the oven is beeping,' he said, reaching up to silence it.

'Oh, sorry, Ruairí,' she said, coming to. 'I never even heard it.'

He rested his back against the counter top. 'You're miles away.'

'I'm just really worried for Tadgh,' she admitted, turning around to face him.

'If you're anxious, why don't you go and give him a hand? I'll be okay here.'

'But what about the lunchtime rush? They'll start arriving any minute.'

'I'll manage. So what if the queue moves a little slower?' He shrugged. 'It's only for one day.'

Penny's face lit up. 'Would you mind? I think he'd really appreciate it, even if it's just for moral support.'

'Not at all.'

'Thanks, Ruairí.' Penny quickly unhooked her apron from around her neck and gave him a peck on the cheek. 'I promise I'll make it up to you.'

'Good luck. I'll have everything crossed for him,' he called after her, but she had already run out the door.

21

Grace was standing on a stool, reaching up to dust the tall shelves of the dresser, enjoying the clarity of mind that cleaning always gave her, while Maggie sat in front of her easel. Grace had called over to Cavendish Hall several more times over the last few days, and she and Patrick were getting to know one another. It was strange to look at him and see her features – like the way his nose sloped upwards at the tip, and the angular slant to his forehead. Once they had got over the tension of their initial meeting, she was surprised to find that they got on well together. Patrick, although naturally shy and reserved, had a quirky sense of humour. He also had a tendency not to get caught up in day-to-day stresses and lived a very simple life. For all the grandeur of Cavendish Hall, there were no airs and graces about him, which Grace found refreshing.

She knew it had been difficult for Maggie to see her and Patrick spending time getting to know one another. Grace was excited to discover more about her father, but she also knew how suspicious Maggie was of him, so her loyalties felt torn. Maggie visibly bristled every time Grace mentioned Patrick's name, but Grace believed that if Maggie just listened to Patrick's side of the story, then she would see things in a new light. Perhaps one day they could even finally put all those years of anger behind them. If she had any hope of establishing a relationship with her father, she needed to have Maggie on board. She just wanted everyone to get along.

She put down her cleaning rag and took a deep breath before asking her aunt the question she been trying to work up the courage to ask all morning.

'Maggie?' she began.

'Yes,' her aunt replied, not looking up from the canvas.

'Patrick has invited us over for tea,' Grace said. She was trying to sound casual, but she wasn't sure she was pulling it off.

'Patrick?' Maggie asked, sticking her head around the side of the easel.

'Yes, he thinks it would be good for us all to get to know one another better...'

Maggie put down her paintbrush and pushed her stool out from behind the easel so she could look directly at Grace. 'I already know Patrick Cavendish, and I don't like the man,' she said bluntly.

'Please, Maggie,' Grace begged.

'Ah, Grace, come on now. You go and have tea with him if you want. You don't need me there like some kind of chaperone.'

'But I want you to see the place.'

'I'm sorry, Grace. I wouldn't be able to hold my tongue. No, you're better off without me.'

'Come on, Maggie, just hear him out. I really want you to meet him – I could use your support.'

'Ah, Grace, it's going to be fierce awkward.' Maggie shook her head.

Disappointment flooded through Grace. She knew Maggie would never forget Rosa's pain and heartbreak all those years ago, but she was sure that if her aunt just gave Patrick a chance to tell his side of the story, she'd see that he wasn't the monster she had believed him to be for all these years.

'Ah, Grace, don't make that face,' Maggie warned her.

'What face?' Grace asked faux-innocently. She knew that Maggie couldn't bear it when Grace looked disappointed. When she was a little girl and Rosa wouldn't allow her to have sweets in O'Herlihy's, Maggie always bought them for Grace and passed them to her whenever Rosa wasn't looking because she said she hated seeing her sad face.

'Oh, all right then.' Maggie sighed, resigned. 'But you needn't think we're all going to suddenly start playing happy families. It's not an episode of *Long Lost Families*.'

Grace risked a smile. 'Just give him a chance,' she pleaded.

'I'll be on my best behaviour.' Maggie scowled.

~

'Wow, look at you,' Grace said when Maggie emerged from the bedroom on her crutches later that afternoon. Her ankle was improving every day and she was slowly starting to bear weight on it.

Maggie began to blush, feeling self-conscious. 'Is it too much?' she asked, smoothing down the forest-green knit dress she had chosen. She had looped a magenta scarf around her neck and had put on gold earrings. She had spent a long time dithering over what to wear and Grace could tell she was nervous. Her aunt had even applied make-up, something she never usually wore.

'No, you look beautiful. I'm not used to seeing you like this, that's all.'

When they were ready, they got into Grace's Mini Cooper and set off for Cavendish Hall.

'Imagine, all my life living in Inishbeg Cove and I've only ever seen the place once,' Maggie said as they drove through the village. She told Grace how, as a child, a few of them had dared each other to cycle down the avenue leading to Cavendish Hall, but that was the first and last time she had set eyes on the house.

'Really?' Grace was surprised. The more she learnt about the big house, the more it seemed that the Cavendish family had kept themselves locked away in their ivory tower and hadn't mixed with the villagers.

'I remember my mother telling me that Patrick's grandmother, who would be your great-grandmother, used to hold a mulled wine reception for the villagers every Christmas, but when Patrick's parents inherited the estate, they stopped all of that.'

Grace thought about her paternal grandparents. She didn't like the picture that had been painted of them so far. They sounded ruthless and cold-hearted. Even Patrick didn't speak about his parents with any great warmth or affection.

She turned the car through the elegant acorn-topped pillars, and they bumped over the potholes that pitted the driveway. Eventually when they rounded the final bend, the house came into view. In the passenger seat, she saw Maggie taking in the grandeur of the house. Grace was still trying to wrap her head around the fact that one day it would all be hers.

'Are you ready?' Grace asked, parking then climbing out of the car. Maggie hobbled over towards the door, gravel crunching underfoot. Grace led the way through the pillars framing the portico and helped Maggie up the steps. Then she rapped the knocker. Patrick answered almost instantly, as if he had been waiting for them.

'Grace, Maggie.' He smiled. 'I'm so pleased you came.'

They followed him through to the drawing room, where Grace had sat on her first visit to the house. Maggie was drawn to the long windows with their views of the sea. She walked over and looked out over the slate-grey Atlantic water.

'It's spectacular, isn't it?' Patrick said, coming up behind her. 'I've lived here my whole life, and I never tire of it. My great-great-great-grandfather William Cavendish built this house as a summer retreat for his wife Eliza, but Eliza loved it here so much, it ended up becoming the family's main residence. Anyway, enough of the history lesson. Let me get the tea. I bought some scones in Ruairí's earlier – will you have one?'

'It looks as though he's a one-man band,' Maggie muttered when Patrick had left the room. 'I thought he'd have a housekeeper, at least. How on earth does he keep a house of this size on his own?'

'He only has Donie helping him on the farm, apparently.'

'I can't believe Donie Fahey still works here!' Maggie was clearly surprised. 'He nearly lost his job after Patrick's parents learnt he had been the one who introduced their son to Rosa. The only reason they kept him on was because Donie's father John threatened to leave if Donie lost his job. John was an excellent farm manager, by all accounts, and the Cavendish family knew they'd never be able to replace him.'

Maggie tipped back her head and looked up at the intricate plasterwork decorating the high ceilings. Although there was no denying its beauty, the plaster had started to fall away and the damask wallpaper was peeling from the walls, leaving shiny, damp patches beneath. It really was a pitiful sight.

'Look at the dust on those paintings.' Maggie tutted. 'And that's saying something coming from me!'

Grace laughed. 'I'm itching to give it a good clean.'

Patrick returned to the room after a few minutes and poured the tea into mismatched china teacups. Then he took a seat on the Chesterfield opposite them.

'I want to thank you, Maggie,' Patrick began. 'For telling Grace the truth. I've waited so many years to meet her, and I have to say she is every bit as charming and delightful as I had imagined. Her mother did a remarkable job raising her.'

'She did,' Maggie agreed. 'Patrick, I want to ask you if what Grace said is true. Did you try to make contact with Rosa and Grace over the years?' Although Rosa had never told Maggie that Patrick had been in contact, Maggie knew better than anyone how stubborn Rosa could be once she had made up her mind about something.

'Many times,' he said sadly, 'but she always returned my letters. After Grace was born, I called to the cottage where she stayed with you that summer. I asked if I could meet her but Rosa told me never to contact her again, and I had to respect her wishes. I wrote to Grace every year on her birthday and at Christmas, but my letters were always returned unopened. It was no more than I deserved, though.'

'She had her reasons. How could you do it to her, Patrick?' Maggie went on. 'You fooled her – you fooled us all! Rosa was devastated.'

'I loved Rosa more than you will ever know. I really thought my parents would come round to the idea of us being together. Then one day I got Rosa's letter and I was so confused. I couldn't understand why she was ending things between us. It was only during Grace's recent visit that I learnt the truth about what my mother and Tabitha had done to her. If I could turn back the clock, I would do everything differently...' he said wistfully. 'Tell me, did she ever meet another man?'

Maggie shook her head. 'You were the only man she ever loved. She closed her heart to love the day you left her, Patrick.'

'She was my only love too.'

Maggie raised her brows cynically. 'And what about Tabitha? You seemed in an awful hurry to get up the aisle with her!'

'It was all arranged by my parents. When Rosa cut off contact with me, I was devastated. I didn't have the fight left in me, so I gave in to their wishes. They threw a lavish engagement party and it was full steam ahead with the wedding plans. But I didn't love Tabitha, and I don't think she ever loved me. I'll never forgive myself for my actions. And what was it all for? Look at me now, living on my own in my big old house. I don't deserve any sympathy, but I often think how much happier my life would have been if I had followed my heart and stopped waiting for my parents' permission. For all these years, I've done my duty by my family and to Cavendish Hall, but now it's time for me to do right by my daughter. It will all be Grace's soon.' He gestured around the room.

Maggie seemed taken aback. Grace realised that she hadn't expected him to be so forthright.

'So what Grace mentioned about inheriting the estate – you're serious about it?' Maggie asked. 'You're not just saying it to sweeten her up?'

'Of course I'm not. It's gifted to Grace in my will, but now that I've found her, it's hers whenever she wants it. I'll gladly sign the paperwork and hand it over to her to do whatever she likes with it.'

'But where will you live?' Grace asked, still dumbfounded by the whole thing.

'I can live out my days in the dower house on the grounds. It'll be far easier to heat than this place.'

'And what about the gift tax she would be liable for? Where is she supposed to get the money to cover that?' Maggie retorted.

'Well obviously I wouldn't want Grace to bear that burden so I have a financial policy in place to cover that,' Patrick explained.

'But what will Grace *do* with this place?' Maggie continued in bewilderment. 'A house like this could break your heart. It's a lot for a young woman to take on, especially a woman who doesn't have a few million quid sitting in the bank.'

'Actually, I've been thinking—' Grace interrupted.

'Go on,' Patrick said, smiling encouragingly at her.

Grace took a deep breath. She had mulled this over in her mind so often over the last few days. In her head it seemed like a good idea; she just hoped it didn't sound ridiculous as soon as she said it out loud. 'I've given it a lot of thought,' she began, 'and houses like this can't be sustained without an income. The sad truth is, this house needs to be a business if we're to have any hope of saving it, so I was thinking ... perhaps we could turn it into a boutique hotel. You know, an exclusive wedding venue, or we could hold small concerts here, that kind of thing.'

Silence fell upon them and Grace wondered if her plan had sounded ludicrous when she said it out loud. She swallowed hard before continuing. 'Inishbeg Cove has no hotels, even though tourist numbers are growing steadily every year. We could even convert the stable block into extra bedrooms to give us more flexibility for guests when we have events on.'

She had lain in bed the previous night growing excited as the idea had taken hold in her head. But what did she know about running a hotel? Or restoring an old house? She knew her creative eye would help with the interiors and choosing finishes, but that was only a very small part of the overall plan.

'I like it,' Patrick said eventually, after he had considered what she had said. 'What a marvellous idea, Grace.'

'Hang on, just slow down a minute,' Maggie interjected. 'As great an idea as it is, how on earth are you going to get the money to do something like that? I know the house is beautiful, and with the right restoration it would make a wonderful hotel, Grace, but you'd need to spend hundreds of thousands, maybe millions, before you could open your doors.'

'Maggie's right,' Patrick admitted. 'Every little job in this house is extortionate. I had a leak repaired here last year and I still sweat every time I think about the cost. Then another pipe sprang a leak a few weeks later. The income generated from the farm is a pittance, after I pay Donie, it barely gives me a wage. I have a few paintings I can sell to raise money, but that wouldn't come to anything near what we would need. I've sold off so much of the contents over the years to fund repair work, there's not much left of any value, to be honest.'

'Well, I hope I'm not getting ahead of myself, but I did a bit of googling over the last few days, and it seems there are a few government grants we can apply for to help with the restoration costs. Also, if we agree to open the house to the public a few days a year, we can benefit from certain tax breaks.'

'You are a clever girl,' Patrick said, looking at her in admiration.

Maggie tutted. 'Grace, you and I both know that a government grant wouldn't even cover filling the potholes in the driveway!'

Grace took a deep breath to prepare herself for what she was about to say next. 'I know that ... so I was also thinking of selling the house in Ranelagh.'

'You can't do that!' Maggie was aghast.

'I can't see me ever returning to the house without Mum being there. It will be too painful; it's not home without her.' Grace had known that Maggie wouldn't be receptive to the idea, so she had all her reasons ready.

'I know, love, but even if you stay with me in Inishbeg Cove for the rest of your life, the house in Dublin is your security, just in case anything should ever happen. It was very important to your mother that you wouldn't have any financial worries after she was gone. I can't let you sell it, Grace.' She shook her head resolutely. 'No way.'

'I know it's a gamble, but I've thought about it a lot. It's the first time in years that I've actually been excited about something. I couldn't sleep last night thinking about what I could do with this place. Accountancy isn't for me. I've known that for a while now, but I was always afraid to take a risk and follow my heart. Look, at this place–' she gestured around the room. '–it's beautiful and I'm bursting with ideas about what I can do with it. Now I finally have a chance to do something I'm passionate about – I really want to make this work.'

'But even selling the house in Ranelagh won't give you enough to cover the amount of work that has to be done here,' Maggie countered.

'Well, I could go to the bank with a business plan. I'm pretty sure that if I could front half the money, the bank would match it, if I had a sound financial case.'

'Grace, I have to say I agree with Maggie,' Patrick interrupted. 'If your mother left her house to you as security for the future, I couldn't ask you to risk it on this place. That wouldn't sit right with me at all.'

Maggie sat back in her chair and her shoulders relaxed as she exhaled heavily. Grace could tell she was relieved that she and Patrick were on the same page.

'Well, I could put the house up as security and get a business loan against it. I probably couldn't borrow as much that way, but perhaps we could do it in stages. I could get the work done to the rooms that would be used by a wedding party and hotel guests. We could hold off on the stable wing until the business is profitable and we can fund the renovations ourselves. How does that sound?'

'It's risky,' Maggie said cautiously, 'but I can see how excited you are about it so I think it's a fair compromise.'

'Patrick, what do you think?' Grace turned to him.

'I think you're just marvellous, Grace!' He beamed.

'She got that from our side,' Maggie quipped, and they all laughed.

22

Penny ran up along the cliff path and by the time she reached the restaurant, she was out of breath. She pushed on the arched door and hurried inside. Tadgh was washing the floor. He looked up, and his face lit up when he saw her. 'What are you doing here?' he asked in disbelief, resting his weight on the handle of the mop.

'I thought...' – she stopped to catch her breath – 'you could use some moral support.'

'But what about the café?'

'It was Ruairí's idea. He said he'll manage without me for today.'

Tadgh left the mop, came over and took her in his arms. Then he planted a kiss on her lips. 'I don't think I've ever been as glad to see you. I haven't been this nervous since the first service I did alone at eighteen.'

Penny rubbed his arm. 'I have faith in you. Just be honest and the truth will win out, I'm sure of it. So what can I do to help?'

'Could you go through the cupboards and make sure

they're all in order? I want to check over the temperature log for the fridges and finish washing the floor.'

They were hard at work when they heard a knock a while later. They knew it was the inspector. Penny mouthed 'good luck' to Tadgh, then he opened the door to find a woman dressed in a formal business suit standing before him.

'Are you Mr Tadgh O'Reilly?' she began.

He nodded.

'I'm Jenny McGovern. I'm an environmental health officer for the Midwest region. As you are aware, you are being investigated for an alleged food poisoning incident which took place in your restaurant recently. I'd like to start with a visual inspection of the premises, and then I will check your records, so please have them ready. After that I will ask you some questions, if that's okay. Now, I'd like to start with the kitchen.'

'Sure,' Tadgh said, standing aside to let her in, his heart thumping. 'It's this way.'

Penny and Tadgh watched anxiously as the inspector made her way around the restaurant with her clipboard. She lifted jars to read their labels; she opened cupboards to examine the contents, periodically making notes on her clipboard.

'What do you think she's writing?' Tadgh whispered, his eyes following every step the inspector took.

'Try not to worry,' Penny replied. She was doing her best to allay his fears, but failing to disguise the worry in her own voice.

They watched the woman as she worked her way around the kitchen. Eventually she made her way over to them. 'Now then, that's the visual inspection completed. I will need your hygiene inspection logs, your temperature records, your HACCP plan and all your staff training records.'

'Of course,' Tadgh said, going over to the shelf where he kept the folders with all his records. He was grateful that he kept his paperwork up to date. He knew many chefs that weren't so meticulous; they hated having to deal with the boring details of running a restaurant, but now Tadgh could see why they were important. He took down the folders and brought them over to her. Jenny McGovern sat down at a table and began to scrutinise them, flicking through their pages and making more notes. She seemed to be going through everything with a fine-tooth comb.

'All your records appear to be up to date. If you don't mind, I have a few questions that I need to ask you,' she said eventually. 'Please take a seat.'

Tadgh and Penny did as the inspector suggested, and the three of them sat at a table.

'I see your supplier list is mainly local producers' – she read from her notes – 'except for your crab claws, which I believe are caught by you personally.'

'There is a shelf in the cove where they gather and I swim out to get them. We are famous for our crab – not just in Inishbeg Cove, but in the entire county and beyond,' Tadgh said passionately. 'We've been catching our own crabs and preparing them in the same way for generations. My grandparents did it that way, then my parents before me, and they taught me how to do it.'

'But you are not an officially registered supplier,' Jenny probed.

'Well, no … but they're the freshest crabs you will find because there is no supply chain – they come straight from the Atlantic Ocean that day and are served in my restaurant that night.'

'That's all well and good, but if you are both the supplier and the chef, then no one else is accountable for the traceability of the supply chain or the quality of the food that is being served to customers,' Jenny stated.

Tadgh felt wounded. Was she trying to insinuate that it was the crab that had caused the alleged food poisoning? She could blame anything else – but not the crab. 'My crab is always served to the highest standards,' he said with unwavering conviction.

'On the 16th of November last, the complainant said they ate crab claws here,' the inspector began. 'It was the only dish they ate that night. The complainant can remember thinking the crab claws tasted funny, but assumed it was because they were seafood. It wasn't until they returned home that they started to feel unwell, and they realised that the crab must have been off.'

Hope flickered inside Tadgh. 'But they couldn't have,' he said quickly, eager to get the words out. 'We didn't have crab claws on the menu that night.'

Jenny raised her brows doubtfully. 'How can you remember so easily?'

'Because we haven't had crab on the menu in over three months. I've been recovering from an accident so I haven't been up to catching them. I could buy crabs in the market or from a *registered supplier*,' he emphasised the words, 'but they wouldn't be as fresh as the ones I cook, so I preferred to leave them off the menu rather than serve them under par.'

The inspector eyed him suspiciously. 'You have a restaurant which you say is famous for its crab, yet you have left it off the menu for the last three months?' she said disbelievingly.

'Wait!' Penny cried, jumping up.

Tadgh and the inspector turned to look at her. 'What is it?' Tadgh asked.

'You can check his diary,' Penny said, feeling a surge of hope. They could prove to the inspector that Tadgh was being set up! She crossed the room, went behind the reception desk and returned with the black leather-bound menu-planning diary that Tadgh used to plan his dishes and the ingredients required. Penny had often seen him sitting at the kitchen table at home with it as he prepared for the week ahead.

Jenny McGovern began to flick through the pages. She finally stopped at the date in question and looked up at him. 'I can see that crab hasn't featured on your menu in over three months, like you said.'

'That's correct.'

The inspector nodded. 'Well, from what I've seen today, this is a well-run, clean establishment. Not all places I inspect have standards like this. Since the complainant refused to provide a stool sample, I have to wonder if there is a vexatious element at play here.'

'Really?' Tadgh asked, daring to hope.

'I am satisfied with the outcome of my inspection today. We won't be proceeding any further with the investigation, Mr O'Reilly.'

'That's it?' Tadgh was stunned. 'It's all over?'

'That's it,' Jenny said, standing up and shaking his hand. 'I wish you all the best.' She began to gather up her belongings.

'Oh, thank God.' Penny sagged with relief and threw her arms around Tadgh as soon as the inspector had left. Although he wrapped her in his arms, she thought his reaction seemed a little muted, and pulled back to study his face. 'What's wrong, Tadgh?'

He exhaled heavily. 'Don't get me wrong. Of course I'm happy and relieved, but this just proves that someone is out to get me. Until we find out who's behind all of this, I feel like a sitting duck. They've already gone to great lengths to destroy me – what will they do next? How much further will they go?'

23

The low buzz of chatter hummed between the café walls, punctuated periodically by the grind and choke of the coffee machine. The door opened and Tadgh and Penny came in, holding hands.

'Well?' Ruairí asked. 'I'm guessing by your smiles that it went okay?'

'It did, but it looks like our friend the Undercover Critic has been at it again,' Tadgh announced, anger blistering his words.

'I knew it!' Ruairí cried. 'Come on, don't keep me in suspense. What happened?'

'So the person who claimed to have food poisoning said they had eaten crab on the night in question – but Tadgh hasn't had crab on the menu since before his accident, as he hasn't been able to catch them!' Penny said breathlessly as she filled Ruairí in. She could still hardly believe that someone was trying so hard to sabotage his restaurant.

'Whoever is behind this is starting to slip up,' Ruairí said. 'Mark my words, we're getting closer to finding out who they are.'

'But what are they going to do next?' Tadgh asked, his voice heavy with desperation. 'How much further are they willing to go? Writing a newspaper review, faking a landslide and a food poisoning incident are kind of a big deal.'

'Let's forget about the Undercover Critic for a moment,' Ruairí said, 'because for now, we are celebrating! I wish I had something stronger to give you, but coffee will have to do. I'll give you a double shot.'

'You're too wild!' Tadgh laughed as he and Penny removed their coats and sat down at a table. After a few minutes Ruairí brought three coffees and a selection of cakes to the table. There was a rich chocolate brownie, a frangipane tartlet, slices of moist banana loaf and, of course, his signature fluffy lemon drizzle cake. Because it was nearly closing time, the café was quiet, so he was able to join them.

'What's all this?' Maggie tutted as she entered the café a few minutes later with two paintings wrapped up in brown paper, tucked beneath her arm. 'Are you skiving again, Ruairí?'

'Can't a man rest for five minutes?' Ruairí sighed in pretend exasperation. 'Good to see you back on your feet again, Maggie. Sit down,' he ordered, pulling out a chair for her. 'What can I get you?'

'Tea for me, thanks, and a scone if you're buying.' Maggie winked as she set down the paintings and took off her coat, joining them at the table.

'I heard you'd been in the wars.' Tadgh nodded at her ankle. 'How are you doing?'

'*Aragh*, I was just being my usual clumsy old self. I went over on it during a swim. Thankfully Liam was able to get me out of the water, or it might have ended very differently.'

'Finally, someone with an accident more dramatic than mine.' Tadgh grinned.

'At least you're off your crutches now,' Penny remarked through a bite of her tartlet, savouring the almondy sweetness.

'I've been a good girl and have done all the exercises the physio gave me. I'm allowed back swimming soon too.'

'That'll be good – you must have missed it,' Tadgh said.

'You've no idea. I've never painted so much. I was like a woman possessed with the brush.'

'So where's Grace?' Ruairí asked as he brought Maggie's tea and scone down to the table.

'She just dropped me off. We were over in Cavendish Hall earlier.'

'What on earth were you doing there?' Ruairí was surprised.

'Well, where do I start?' They all sat there, riveted, as Maggie filled them in on the whole saga about Patrick Cavendish being Grace's father and how she was set to inherit the estate. 'She's gone back home to work on her business plan. I've never seen her so enthusiastic about anything before.'

'Oh, that sounds exciting!' Penny said. 'The very best of luck to her.'

The foursome were sitting around chatting and laughing when the door opened again and Liam entered, his laptop bag slung over his shoulder.

'Liam!' Maggie called to him. 'Will you join us for a cuppa?'

'Oh, go on then, just a quick one,' he said. 'I promised myself that I'd write a thousand words today, come hell or high water, and I've only managed around a hundred so far.' He groaned. 'I thought the change of scenery in the café might help.'

'I think we all owe you an apology,' Penny began sheepishly as Liam sat down at the table. 'We thought you were the person giving Tadgh a hard time.'

'Maggie filled me in on that dreadful business. I can see why you thought it was me. Did you get to the bottom of it yet?'

Tadgh shook his head glumly. Although he was relieved that the inspection had gone to plan and he was finally able to open the restaurant again to salvage what was left of his business, he couldn't shake the unease that he was waiting for the Undercover Critic to strike again. He felt like a chess piece in a game being controlled by someone else; he was just waiting for the next move to be played.

'What can I get you?' Ruairí asked.

'I'll have a tea, please, Ruairí and one of those pear and almond scones would be lovely.'

Ruairí stood up and made his way towards the counter once more while Liam began to root around in his pocket for his wallet.

'Put your wallet away, it's my treat,' Tadgh said.

'There's really no need,' Liam insisted.

'It's the least I can do to apologise for the mix-up, and to thank you for saving our darling Maggie.' He leant in towards Liam. 'I would have left her there,' he teased in a stage whisper.

Maggie elbowed Tadgh playfully.

'So, how's the ankle?' Liam asked, turning to Maggie.

'It's getting stronger. Actually what are you doing on Monday morning around eleven?'

'Nothing – why?'

'I might need you on standby, Mitch,' she said with a laugh. 'I'm allowed to head back into the water. Will you join us for a swim?'

He shook his head playfully and grinned at her. 'You can find another lifeguard, Maggie O'Neill!'

'Ah, come on, Liam. We're a lovely bunch, honest to God, and even if you hate it, there will be a nice warm cuppa and a biscuit waiting for you afterwards.'

He pushed a lock of salt-and-pepper coloured hair out of his eyes. 'We'll see,' he said.

~

ON MONDAY MORNING Maggie and Grace made their way across the blonde sand towards the other swimmers. Although Maggie was nervous, she was mainly looking forward to immersing herself in the cool Atlantic water and catching up with her friends. She had sorely missed her daily sea-swims while she had been out of action. The sunshine and azure sky couldn't hide the dip in temperature since the day she had last ventured into the water. The sea, like a sheet of shimmering silver, was the calmest she had seen it in a long time; only the gentlest of waves broke on the shore as it waited to welcome her back.

In the distance she saw an outline she didn't recognise, standing on the fringes of the group near the rocks. It was only as she got closer that she realised it was Liam. She hurried across the sand towards him.

'You came?' she asked, sounding shocked, when she reached him.

He grinned at her. 'You said you needed a lifeguard.'

'Everyone, I want to introduce you to Liam. This is the man that saved my life.'

'You're a real hero, by all accounts,' Frank, one of the swimmers, said.

Liam shifted awkwardly. Maggie knew he was uncomfortable being the centre of attention.

'I just did what anyone would have done,' he said modestly.

'So it wasn't enough that you saved her life, now she's dragged you along for a swim too?' Laura joked.

'Maggie can be very persuasive,' Liam said.

'You mean she doesn't take no for an answer,' Grace quipped.

Maggie shook her head at the teasing. 'Come on then, you lot,' she called, rubbing her hands together. 'No point standing around getting cold – let's show Liam what he's been missing.'

The group began to unpeel their clothes, unzipping coats and pulling down leggings. As Liam pulled his sweater over his head, Maggie noticed that he was in good shape. She was so used to seeing him with his coat on or in big woolly jumpers in the café that she was surprised to find he had a nicely toned chest and strong arms beneath the layers.

'Are you ready?' she asked when he had stripped down to his swimming shorts.

'As ready as I'll ever be.' He grimaced as they walked across the rippled sand towards the water's edge.

Grace waded in quickly, but Maggie gasped as the shock of cold water stung her bootie-clad feet.

'Come on, Maggie, mind over matter. No pain, no gain,' Grace teased, quoting the motivational mantras that Maggie was so fond of quoting to other people whenever they were prolonging their entrance into the water.

Maggie clenched her jaw and kept going. The water was colder than it had been the last time she swam, but she knew there was no easy way through this; she just had to get it over with. Once the endorphins started flowing, she would reap the benefits. She was careful with her ankle, choosing her steps carefully in case there were any sudden drops. Looking over, she saw that Liam was already thigh-deep. Grace was lying back, floating, letting the gentle waves lift her before they continued to roll towards the shore.

Once Liam and Maggie were in deep enough, they lay back in their salty bath, using their arms to keep themselves afloat while the others began to swim parallel to the shore. For those few minutes the shock of the cold water meant that Maggie could switch off from everything else; all that mattered was the buoyant sea keeping her afloat and the vast sky above.

When the cold began to bite mere minutes later, the swimmers began to emerge from the sea. They dried off in the bowl of the cove, protected from the onshore winds by the looming cliffs that sheltered the horseshoe-shaped bay. Fishing boats bobbed happily on their moorings as if they too were enjoying the glorious blue-sky Inishbeg Cove day.

'I feel like a new woman after that,' Maggie exclaimed, briskly towelling her goosebump-dotted arms. It was as though she had left her troubles behind her in the water and she had emerged a lighter person. 'What did you think, Liam?'

Droplets of water shone like crystals in his hair and his face was ruddy from the cold, but his smile told her everything. 'It was good,' he said through chattering teeth as he dried himself. 'Baltic, but good.'

'Here, have a coffee to warm up,' she offered when they were finished dressing. Steam rushed out onto the air as she opened her thermos flask and poured him a mug, then another for herself. She always carried extra mugs in her backpack in case anyone in the group was short. He took it gladly from her and curled his hands around it, savouring its warmth.

'Would you like a biscuit?' she asked.

'I won't say no.'

She rooted in her bag, took out a packet of ginger nuts and handed it to him. He used his thumbs to push one up before passing the pack along to the next person.

'I must say, it's great to have some new members in our little group,' Maggie remarked to Liam while the rest of the group chatted. 'Usually people cry off in the colder weather, and the holiday-home owners go back to their own lives when summer is over. To be honest, it's been me on my tod for the last few winters, so it's lovely to have company on the cold mornings. You'll have to bring Ingrid along when she comes down to visit,' Maggie went on. 'Now that you've taken the plunge yourself, if you'll pardon the pun.' She laughed at her own joke but suddenly Liam's gaze darted away and the air changed between them.

'What is it? Oh dear, what did I say?' Maggie implored.

'Oh – I... eh ... well ... Ingrid passed away six years ago.'

'Heavens above!' Maggie's hands flew to her mouth. 'I'm so sorry. Me and my big gob! I'm always putting my foot in it.'

'It's not your fault. Sorry, I thought I had told you,' Liam said apologetically. 'Didn't you wonder why she was never with me?'

'I just assumed she was in Dublin while you were down here to write.'

'Sometimes I talk about her like she's still alive, so I'm sorry if you got the wrong end of the stick,' he said wistfully.

'My sister Rosa died recently, and I do the same thing. It's hard to believe that the person you loved beyond words is no longer around.' She smiled sadly at him. 'How did Ingrid die?'

'She fought a valiant battle with early onset dementia.'

'That's awful, Liam.'

'It was tough, I won't lie, but whenever we came to Inishbeg Cove, she was happy and she had many good days down here. We would come here just to escape from it all. I don't know what it was about this place – maybe it was because she had spent so many happy childhood summers down here, or perhaps it was the sea air – but her mind always seemed a little clearer when she was here, so I have lots of fond memories to treasure. It's a very special place.'

Maggie reached across and gave Liam's hand a quick squeeze. 'It is,' she agreed. 'So, will we see you at same time again tomorrow?'

Liam dipped his ginger nut into his coffee, then grinned at her. 'I'll bring the biscuits.'

24

Maggie stood on the beach in the face of the keen Atlantic wind, her unzipped jacket flapping around her. She had left Grace at home working on her laptop. Grace had made an appointment with the bank manager in Ballymcconnell and was working hard to finalise her business plan for the meeting. Not for the first time, Maggie wondered if Grace had any idea what she was taking on. Maggie realised that, as an accountant, Grace knew her stuff and she trusted her financial judgement, but she still had her doubts about Patrick's intentions. Was he just trying to use Grace as a cash cow to restore his crumbling country pile?

Only the die-hard swimmers like herself had turned up today. The darker mornings and cold weather at this time of year, made the water less appealing, and the number of swimmers coming down to the cove every day was starting to dwindle. People clearly found it too hard to pull themselves out of their warm beds. Maggie had just finished undressing when she saw Liam making his way across the sand towards her.

'We didn't put you off, then?' Maggie shouted to him, the wind sweeping the words from her mouth.

'I have to say, I slept like a baby last night,' he called back, trying to be heard over the cacophony of the raging wind and roaring sea.

'Vitamin sea – you can't beat it.'

'I think you've converted me.' Liam grinned.

Since he had told her the day before that he was a widower, Maggie was looking at Liam in a new light. It was as if he had opened a window inside himself and she was seeing another side to the man. They had connected over their shared grief. They each knew the raw pain of losing someone dear, and the sense of disbelief you felt when you picked up the phone to call them and remembered all over again that they were gone. She realised that Liam probably needed these swims just as much as she did.

They undressed and waded into the sea, allowing the blanket of water to envelop them in a way that was shocking and exhilarating at the same time. As Maggie looked out over the great vastness of the Atlantic Ocean, stretching out endlessly, nothing before her except the sea and sky merging into a teal line on the horizon, she was reminded once again of her place in the world. How we are but a snapshot in time. Her worries or fears were made utterly irrelevant, and she found it strangely reassuring to be reminded of how inconsequential we all are in life's greater plan. She had lost her larger-than-life sister Rosa, yet the waves kept rolling in. Even when you didn't think you could go on, the sun still rose in the morning and the light crept into your bedroom to wake you, and somehow you got out of bed, put your feet on the ground and kept on going.

When they could no longer stand the cold, the swimmers emerged from the water and made their way across the sand to the rock where they had left their belongings. They were glad of the warm embrace of their towels and robes as they dried off.

'So where are the biscuits?' Maggie asked Liam after they had dressed and she had poured them a steaming coffee from her thermos.

'Oh dear...' Liam said, flushing. 'I forgot them.'

'You had one job!' Maggie teased, her hands on her hips.

'Don't worry, I think I might have half a packet of digestives in my bag,' Imelda said, unzipping her backpack and rooting around in its depths.

'Well, you see, I stopped off in O'Herlihy's on my way here,' Liam explained, 'and... eh... something happened, and I forgot all about them... I meant to tell you when I arrived, but it went out of my head completely–'

'Oh yeah?' Maggie asked.

'Now, maybe it's nothing, but I thought it was a bit odd... How about we go for a coffee in Ruairí's instead and I can fill you in?' Liam suggested.

'Ruairí's beats a plain old digestive any day,' Maggie said. She turned to Laura and Imelda. 'Will you join us?'

'I've to go to work,' Laura said, shaking her head.

'And I've an appointment in Ballymcconnell, so I'll have to head off too, unfortunately,' Imelda said.

Liam and Maggie climbed up the path through the dunes and crossed the street to Ruairí's café on their own. They went inside and found the place wasn't too busy, so they managed to get seats in their favourite spot beside the stove. They sat down and warmed their hands over the fire.

'So, what happened in O'Herlihy's?' Maggie asked after Ruairí had brought their coffees and a fruit scone for each of them.

'When I went in earlier to buy the biscuits, I overheard a conversation.'

'Go on,' Maggie urged.

'Well, the man in front of me at the checkout was asking Mrs O'Herlihy about where was good to eat in the area. Normally I wouldn't take any notice of something like that. So Mrs O'Herlihy recommended Tadgh's, but the man said that Tadgh's was overrated and the village really needed a choice of restaurants. Mrs O'Herlihy wasted no time in telling him that Tadgh's was the best restaurant around by a country mile, but then he said – and this is what made my ears prick up: "Well, watch this space!" and he left the shop.'

'Hmm,' Maggie said pensively. 'That does sound strange.'

'It was the way he said it – it sounded like a threat,' Liam continued. 'That's why the biscuits went out of my head. I was wondering – do you think this might be something to do with the Undercover Critic?'

'You think the man you saw in O'Herlihy's could be behind it all?' Maggie asked but, before she could continue, the door opened and Tadgh stormed in, clutching *The Atlantic Times*.

'Speak of the devil,' Maggie muttered. 'Come on.' She beckoned Liam. 'We'd better tell him.'

'Have you seen this?' Tadgh asked, putting the paper down on the counter in front of Penny and Ruairí as Liam and Maggie approached.

'It's not another review, is it?' Ruairí asked.

Tadgh shook his head. 'Apparently the Steak House chain is opening a branch in Inishbeg Cove.'

'Steak House? But why would they want to open a restaurant here?' Maggie was bewildered. She was familiar with the chain: it was a popular, family-friendly restaurant found in most cities and large towns across Ireland, but she would never have imagined a branch opening in Inishbeg Cove. Tadgh had to be mistaken. 'Are you sure, Tadgh?'

'Surely Inishbeg Cove is too small?' Penny agreed.

'That's what I would have thought,' Tadgh said glumly. 'But apparently their fifty-fourth restaurant is going to be here.'

'It's all starting to make sense.' Maggie nodded. 'Liam heard something in O'Herlihy's earlier on—'

They turned to look at him.

'Well, it might be nothing but it did seem a little odd.' Liam filled them in on what the man had said in the shop.

'That's it,' Ruairí said with certainty after Liam had finished. 'My money is on the Steak House chain being behind all of this.'

'But Steak House is a big company – why would they worry about me? I'm small fry compared to them,' Tadgh said, clearly exasperated.

'Maybe, because the village is so small, they're trying to close you down to ensure their own success?' Liam suggested.

'You might be right,' Maggie agreed solemnly. 'But how do we prove that they are mounting an attack against Tadgh?'

'We could find out who owns the chain and confront them?' Liam said.

Tadgh shook his head. 'We need to have proof before we do anything. What if they have nothing to do with it all, it'll look like sour grapes on my part.'

'Tadgh is right,' Ruairí agreed.

'Are we just meant to stand by and wait for them do something else to destroy what is left of his business?' Penny cried.

'Nobody minds a bit of healthy competition, but if the owner is deliberately sabotaging Tadgh to get ahead, that's not fair!' Maggie was equally furious.

'We're close to solving this, Tadgh, I'm sure of it,' Ruairí reassured him. 'Mark my words the Undercover Critic is going to slip up.'

'Well, I'm running out of time,' Tadgh said. 'It's been a week since the council allowed me to reopen but my restaurant has been empty ever since. I had to cancel all my bookings after the business with the landslide, and when I called people to let them know I was back open, some didn't want to rebook because they were annoyed that I had cancelled in the first place. I'm haemorrhaging money. I can't sustain it for much longer. I'll have to start laying off staff if things don't pick up. Three generations of O'Reilly men have run the restaurant, and if I don't get to the bottom of this soon, it's going to end with me.'

25

Maggie stood at the rocks alone and breathed in the briny sea air. It was a bright, sunny, clear winter morning. The blue sky was streaked with vapour trails, and gulls squawked and cawed as they hovered over the fishing boats that were being unloaded at the pier. She had been sorely tempted to stay in bed that morning: the temperature had dropped below freezing overnight, and when Maggie woke she could see her breath in the cool air in her bedroom. Icy crystals laced the windows of the cottage – but she knew that despite the cold-snap, she never regretted a swim once it was done.

She hadn't been able to convince Grace so easily; though; her niece had groaned and turned over in bed when Maggie had tried to wake her, so she had crept out of the room, leaving her to sleep on. The sand sparkled with frost as Maggie walked towards the shore. She guessed the others must have been feeling the same as Grace, as she was the only one there that morning. She decided she'd wait for another few minutes and if nobody showed up, she'd go for a quick dip by herself.

After a while, there was no sign of anyone else coming, so she began to pull her sweatshirt over her head as she started to undress. She shivered when she felt the cold wind bite at her bare skin. Just as she was about to head into the water on her own, she saw Liam making his way towards her. Her heart suddenly picked up speed. *Stop it*, she told herself. Why was her body doing this?

'I thought I was on my tod this morning,' she called out as he got closer.

'Sorry I'm late. Did none of the rest of them come?'

'I think the cold put a lot of people off.'

'They've more sense than we do.' He laughed.

As she watched him undress, she couldn't help but admire his broad, tanned chest.

'Are you ready?' Liam asked when he was finished, then the two of them headed straight for the icy water.

The cold numbed her skin instantly. No matter how many times she did this, the initial stab of the icy water was still a shock. She bent her knees to submerge herself and then she was in. Her arms and legs sliced through the water to keep warm. She turned onto her back and saw Liam grin across at her. They shared a blissful few moments before it was time to return to the shore to warm up.

They stood shuddering on the sand, the only two people in the cove, trying to dry and dress themselves discreetly beneath their robes.

'I was wondering… do you want to come back to mine for some breakfast?' Liam asked as he slid his arms inside his coat. His gaze darted to the sand before he continued, 'Our cottage is only up the road from yours. Sorry…' He paused. 'I still can't get used to saying *my* cottage; I'm so used to referring to everything we shared as ours.'

Maggie placed a gentle hand on his arm. 'Don't worry, I

still do the same with Rosa. Grief is sneaky like that: it's as if your brain can't believe that the person who was such a big part of your life is gone. It still is your cottage – yours and your wife's. It's where your memories are.'

His soft brown eyes twinkled, as a moment of understanding passed between them. 'Thanks, Maggie. So, what do you say?'

'I won't say no. I'm famished,' Maggie said, twining her scarf around her neck, protecting herself from the bitter Atlantic wind.

Maggie and Liam walked out of the village and along the rambling boreen that led up the headland. The sea shimmered and glistened below them and the sky above was washed azure blue. They walked for a short distance uphill, passing Maggie's cottage, before arriving at a pretty, two-storey, whitewashed house that stood just metres from the cliff edge – the result, Maggie knew, of years of coastal erosion.

'Welcome to Sea Spray Cottage,' Liam announced. The cottage was aptly named, thought Maggie: the waves crashing beneath them sent up a spray and she could taste the salt on her lips. She noticed the milky trace of salt crystals on the windows as she followed Liam into the cottage.

Maggie was surprised to see that his home was brightly decorated. The walls were painted turquoise, jewel-coloured cushions littered the red sofa, and throws in shades of emerald and ochre were draped over its back. A dresser painted calamine pink stood at one end of the room, displaying mismatched crockery. Instead of clashing, somehow the different colours worked together. The walls were covered in family photographs – some in colour, some in black and white. Maggie immediately got the sense that it had been a warm and loving home from home for Liam and his family.

She followed Liam through to the kitchen, where he pulled out the frying pan and the meats from the fridge.

'I'll make us a cuppa,' Maggie offered. 'Where do you keep the tea?' She began to open cupboard doors.

'The door on your right,' Liam said as he greased the pan.

Maggie made the tea while Liam fried black pudding, sausages and bacon. When he had cooked their breakfast, he served it up and they sat down at the table.

'Is that Ingrid?' Maggie asked, nodding at a silver-framed photograph that hung on the wall behind Liam. In it was a younger, dark-haired Liam, linking arms with a slender woman in a colourful dress and holding a chubby-cheeked baby.

'It is indeed,' Liam said, cutting into a sausage. 'That's Ultan in her arms.'

'She was very glamorous.'

'She sure was,' Liam said sadly. 'Ingrid loved her style.'

'You haven't changed a bit,' Maggie said, raising a forkful of black pudding to her mouth.

'You're very kind, but I'm a little greyer and pudgier around the middle these days.' Liam laughed. 'What about you, Maggie?'

'What about me?'

'Did you ever marry?' he asked as he buttered a thick slice of soda bread.

'I nearly did, actually. Denis was his name.' She paused. 'I was counting down the days to the wedding ... until I realised he was making a fool of me.'

Denis had humiliated her by leaving her for a girl he worked with, just months before they were due to marry.

Maggie rarely spoke about him; even after all these years, the pain was still as raw as the day she had discovered he was betraying her.

'I'm sorry to hear that.' Liam shook his head. 'Sounds like you had a lucky escape.'

'Ah, look, it was a long time ago. Time heals, as the saying goes.'

'It does,' Liam agreed. 'How's Grace getting on with her father?'

Maggie had filled Liam in on the story about Patrick and told him that Grace was set to inherit Cavendish Hall.

'It's going well so far – they're taking their time and getting to know one another properly. I have to say, despite my initial misgivings, they seem to have really clicked. They spend hours going through their plans for the restoration. It's good to see Grace smiling again.'

'I'm happy for Grace. We'll all have to start calling her Lady Grace of Cavendish Hall from now on,' Liam teased. 'She'll be too posh to mix with the likes of us.'

'I keep slagging her about it; she's not impressed.' Maggie said.

They ate and laughed and drank tea and when the teapot was empty, Liam made another pot for them. 'I must say, this is lovely,' he said, setting the fresh pot down on the table. 'I've always loved cooking, but it's been so long since I've cooked for someone besides myself. I know it's only breakfast, but I had forgotten the simple pleasures of tasty food and good company.'

'Well, I'll go anywhere that someone feeds me.' Maggie grinned as she speared a piece of bacon. 'I'm not fussy.'

'In that case...' Liam began, then hesitated. 'Perhaps you would like to accompany me to Tadgh's for dinner on Friday night?' he asked, looking sheepish.

'That sounds nice. We might be able to round up a few of the others – what do you think?' Maggie suggested.

She watched the heat creep up along Liam's face. He began to twiddle his fork between his middle and index fingers. 'Well, I mean, we can ask them if you want...'

'I thought you meant a sea-swimmers' night out?' Maggie was confused. Had she said something wrong? She was forever putting her foot in stuff...

'Actually, I was hoping perhaps ... it could be just the two of us?' he said tentatively.

Was he suggesting...? No, he couldn't be. It was Maggie's turn to blush as the meaning of his words hit her. Her heart somersaulted and her tummy filled with thousands of butterflies.

'Oh, I see. That would be lovely, Liam. I'd love to join you.' She beamed.

26

Grace's fingers moved deftly over her laptop keys, making a clacking sound as she typed. To Maggie, it seemed her niece had been hunched over her laptop, working night and day on her business plan, ever since she had announced her plans to transform Cavendish Hall into a luxury boutique hotel. Maggie had never seen Grace so enthusiastic about anything before: she was putting her heart and soul into it. Maggie knew it was also a welcome distraction from the loss of her mother. Her niece was determined to make it a success, and Maggie was glad to see glimpses of the old Grace slowly starting to return again.

'There you go, m'lady,' Maggie said, handing Grace a cup of tea and joining her at the table.

'When are you going to get tired of calling me that?' Grace laughed as she pushed aside her laptop and took the mug from Maggie.

'What?' Maggie said, faking confusion. 'I have to address you by your proper title now that you're the lady of the manor. So, how's the business plan coming along?' she asked, nodding towards the laptop.

'Good, so far, I think. I've forecast what I believe are very conservative numbers to begin with.' She bit on her bottom lip. 'I just hope my projections will stand up to scrutiny tomorrow.'

Grace had a meeting with the bank manager in Ballymcconnell the following day. Maggie knew she was nervous. If she didn't get this loan approved, her dreams of transforming Cavendish Hall into a boutique hotel would be over before they had even begun.

To give Patrick his due, he had contacted his solicitor as promised and had begun to transfer the Cavendish Hall estate into Grace's name. Never in a million years had Maggie thought that Patrick would acknowledge Grace as his daughter, let alone leave everything to her. She was still trying to get her head around the news that her niece was going to inherit the estate where her grandmother had once been a servant. Maggie imagined her mother, toiling in the kitchen in Cavendish Hall, beads of sweat lacing her brow as she kneaded pastry, ran to and fro carrying heavy pots, and stirred sauces. Would she ever have imagined that her own granddaughter would be lady of the manor one day? Even Rosa would never have believed that Patrick would leave everything to Grace, Maggie suspected. How she wished Rosa was alive to talk to about it all. Life was mad with its kinks and curves and twists.

Whatever had gone on before, it certainly seemed like Patrick was trying to put the past to right. Not that gifting the estate to Grace could make up for abandoning his pregnant girlfriend and leaving her to raise their daughter alone, but maybe what Grace had said was true: that Patrick had lived his life full of regret and had suffered in his own way.

Patrick was going to accompany Grace to the meeting with the bank manager and Maggie was glad that he was being a support to her. Patrick knew the house intimately, and the extent of the renovations that would need to be undertaken. He told Grace that the house would need to be completely rewired and re-plumbed before it could be turned into a hotel: it would need new windows and a new roof too, and that was before they did any cosmetic work. Maggie gulped every time Grace mentioned something new that she had added to the renovation list. Then they would need to invest in a kitchen suitable for catering events. Maggie came out in a cold sweat every time she thought about the work that Grace had ahead of her; she couldn't imagine how much pressure Grace must be feeling. She really hoped that her niece hadn't bitten off more than she could chew. Everything hinged on the meeting with the bank manager going well tomorrow.

'I won't be here when you get back from the bank tomorrow, but make sure you ring me and let me know how it goes,' Maggie said, taking a sip from her mug.

'Oh?' Grace replied. 'Where are you going?' She wasn't used to her aunt going out anywhere in the evenings. If she did, it was usually with the sea-swimmers, and Grace was invited along too.

'Liam has asked me to go to Tadgh's with him,' Maggie began coyly.

Grace hiked her brows. 'Liam has asked you out on a date?'

'It's not a date, Grace – we're just going for a bite to eat, for heaven's sake!' Maggie blustered, but she could feel her face betray her as she started to blush. The more conscious of it she became, the hotter her face grew.

'It's just the two of you going; he didn't ask me or any of the rest of the swimmers. It sounds like a date to me.'

'It's not like that! Liam has become a very good friend. We enjoy each other's company.'

'You seem to have hit it off,' Grace agreed.

'He's a lovely man,' Maggie said, refusing to be pulled in the direction that Grace wanted to go.

'He's good-looking too,' Grace continued. 'It's as if George Clooney and Bradley Cooper had a love child!'

Maggie howled with laughter and shook her head. 'He's a friend, and that's all it is. Anyway, I'm too old for all of that stuff.'

'You're only fifty, Maggie! You're hardly over the hill.'

'I'm not exactly a teenager, though. I'm too long in the tooth to go through all that again.'

'Aw, Maggie, you're a great catch.' Grace reached across the table and squeezed Maggie's hand. 'I would love for you to meet someone, and I know my mum always hoped you would too.'

'You're too young to remember, Grace, but when Denis left, he took my heart with him.' Maggie shook her head. 'The fecker broke my heart into smithereens. No, Grace, that shop is closed.'

'That was all a long time ago, Maggie. Liam is a good man,' Grace coaxed.

'I'm doing just fine as I am, my dear, thank you very much,' Maggie said, closing down the conversation.

Grace raised her eyebrows at her aunt. 'Are you trying to convince me or yourself?'

Maggie shook her head and got up from the table. She knew Grace had only been joking, but the teasing had needled her. The truth was, Liam's invitation had taken

Maggie by surprise, and she had been asking herself the same questions that Grace had. It had been a long time since a man had shown any interest in her. No matter how much she tried to downplay it, or told herself not to get her hopes up, she couldn't help feeling a frisson of excitement shoot through her every time she thought about Friday night. Maggie had closed the door to love a long time ago, but Liam's invitation had awoken something inside her that she thought had died. The last time she had let love into her heart, it had ended in humiliation and tears. She had sworn then that she'd never let another man do that to her again… but there was something about Liam. He seemed honest and trustworthy, solid and dependable. Was there a chance that something could happen between them? No matter how much she told herself to calm down, she felt like a giddy schoolgirl. Her stomach did a somersault every time she thought about what might be. The sensible part of her brain told her that Liam was probably just looking for companionship. She knew he dearly missed Ingrid. Her heart was running away with itself before her head had had a chance to catch up. She needed to be sensible here. She was ridiculous to think that love could find her at her age, but oh, it was so hard to tell her heart to be careful…

27

Maggie slid the hair grip into her purple curls, but a recalcitrant lock fell in front of her eyes. She tried again, wishing that Grace was there to do her hair for her – but, on second thoughts, she didn't want her niece to see the effort she was making for Liam, so maybe it was for the best that she was getting ready alone.

Grace had left for her meeting with the bank over two hours ago and there had been no word from her. She had promised Maggie that she would let her know as soon as she was finished. Maggie was carrying her phone from room to room as she got ready for dinner, so she wouldn't miss any update from Grace.

When she finally managed to pin back the curl, Maggie stood in front of the mirror to see how she looked. She had dithered all day over what she would wear that evening. She had tried on different trousers and tops then dress after dress until she had finally settled on a mulberry silk dress with long sleeves. The neckline sloped in a gentle V, revealing a hint of cleavage. It was several years since she had worn the dress – the last time had been for Grace's graduation. As she looked at her reflection in the mirror, she wondered if it was too much. She didn't want to look as though she had gone to too much trouble, even though she had.

'You look very elegant, Maggie,' Liam said when she opened the door to him a while later.

She was relieved to see he had made an effort too, and was wearing a jacket and smart trousers. His salt-and-pepper hair was brushed neatly to one side and his brown eyes twinkled. He looked very handsome. She had to admit that Grace was right about him being a cross between George Clooney and Bradley Cooper…

When she was ready, they set off down the headland towards the village. She had worn a pair of flat pumps for the walk. As they made their way along the cliff path that led from the village to Tadgh's, the sea threw up spray against the rocks beneath them. She could feel her hair starting to frizz in the damp air. After all her effort getting ready, she was going to look a right state by the time she got there, she thought.

When they entered the restaurant, Maggie noticed immediately how few diners there were. Normally it was impossible to get a table on a weekend night unless you booked several weeks in advance. It was usually even worse in the run-up to Christmas, but there were plenty of empty tables available.

'It's quiet tonight,' Maggie remarked when Tadgh came over to greet them.

Tadgh nodded. 'It's the middle of December and I have never seen the place so empty,' he said glumly. 'And my reservations in the days up to Christmas aren't looking any better. Only for a few of the locals who have been loyal customers for years, I wouldn't have a sinner in the place.'

'Oh, Tadgh, it's so unfair. Whoever is behind this has really done damage, haven't they, love?' Maggie shook her head as they followed him over to a table and sat down.

'I hate seeing him so worried,' Maggie said to Liam after Tadgh had left them to peruse the menu.

'I know. It's really taking a toll on him,' Liam agreed, reading the wine list.

After a while Tadgh came back to take their orders, and they chatted easily as they waited for their food.

'Sorry, would you mind if I checked my phone?' Maggie said after a few minutes. 'I'm waiting to hear from Grace. She had her meeting with the bank manager this afternoon, but there's still no word from her.' She fished the phone out of her handbag, checked it, then sighed and returned it to her bag.

'Nothing yet?' Liam asked, taking a sip from the Chablis they had chosen from the wine list.

Maggie shook her head.

'Grace is pretty fearless, isn't she?' Liam said. 'Taking on that big old house and trying to make a go of it – it's not for the faint-hearted.'

'That's the beauty of being young; you don't see obstacles and risks. Then suddenly you get older and they start jumping out at you everywhere.'

'Kind of like asking you to come here tonight,' he said tentatively, his eyes studying the tablecloth.

'What do you mean?' She ran her finger through the condensation on the outside of her wine glass.

'Well, I was petrified that you would say no.' He grinned sheepishly at her.

'Why would I do that?' She was genuinely bewildered.

'Well that day on the beach, when you nearly drowned–'

Maggie put a hand up to stop him. 'Don't remind me.' She groaned. She was still embarrassed by her clumsiness.

Just then they were interrupted by Tadgh, arriving with their starters.

'I have the scallops for you, Maggie, and the wild Atlantic cod for you, Liam,' Tadgh said, setting their plates down.

'Thanks, Tadgh,' they replied. 'It looks great.'

'Sorry, where were we?' Maggie asked when Tadgh had departed.

'I was just about to say that I'm so glad I met you, even if the circumstances weren't the best.'

'You can say that again,' Maggie agreed.

'I really enjoy being around you, Maggie,' he continued. 'You're a breath of fresh air.'

'Oh, thank you.' She blushed and looked down at the stone floor, touched.

'Recently I've started to feel hopeful again,' Liam said. 'For the first time since Ingrid died, I'm actually looking forward to the future. I was trying to work out what had changed...'

'And did you figure it out?' Maggie asked, as she cut down into a scallop with her knife and fork before raising a piece to her mouth.

Heat crept along Liam's face. 'Well, I realised it all started to happen around the time I met you.'

'I see,' Maggie mumbled. Her mouth was too full to talk properly. Why could she never be graceful like other women? she thought.

'I hope I'm not out of line to say that I find you very attractive.' Liam smiled at her. Maggie felt her cheeks grow warm and the scallop seemed to be taking an eternity to chew. He had used the word 'attractive' to describe her. Her.

Maggie knew she was no oil painting. She was overweight; her hair was frizzy and currently purple; she never usually bothered with her appearance. Yet Liam found something attractive in her.

'Thank you,' she muttered, the scallop finally swallowed.

'Is that all you're going to say?' Liam seemed disappointed.

'Sorry. I just wasn't expecting that.' She was at a loss for words for the first time in her life.

'I love your energy and spark, Maggie. You're so comfortable in your own skin – it's refreshing.'

Maggie was stunned. She felt her heart start to beat a little faster and tiny bubbles of excitement filled her tummy. 'No one has ever said that to me before,' she admitted.

'I know when you get to our age it's a bit tricky, but if you were willing, I'd like to explore where this goes, whether that's friendship or perhaps even romance. What do you think?'

Maggie grinned. 'I think I'd like that very much, Liam.'

~

GRACE AND PATRICK emerged from the oppressive interior of the bank and stepped out into the darkness of Ballymcconnell main street. Dusk had fallen, and the only light came from the colourful Christmas lights that were strung from lamppost to lamppost. Grace was exhausted and her head was thumping. The meeting had gone on for far longer than she had expected. She checked her watch and saw it was almost seven o'clock. They had been in the office for over three hours as the bank manager had pulled apart her plan, line by line, and grilled her on how she had arrived at her projections.

'Well,' Grace said, turning nervously to Patrick as soon as they were a safe distance away from the bank. 'How do you think it went?'

'Grace, you were a marvel in there. Every time they came at you with another problem, you were ready and able for them. I'm so proud of you. I felt as though I was watching a James Bond assassin taking down bad guys.' He made shooting noises.

'Thank you, Patrick. I was a bag of nerves.'

'Really?' He looked shocked. 'I never would have guessed. You must be a good actress. I thought you were remarkably composed, all things considered. You reminded me so much of your mother in there – you have the same fighting spirit.'

'It wasn't all me. You stood up to your fair share of questioning too. You lost me, though, when you started talking about plaster cornicing and the intricacies of Georgian plumbing.' Grace laughed.

'I think I lost everyone.' Patrick laughed too. 'Well, it's in the lap of the gods now. No matter what happens, we've done our best. Even if they turn us down, I feel like I've already won.' He smiled genially at her. 'I must say, I'm enjoying getting to know you so much and catching up on all those years I missed.'

'Me too.' She smiled back at him as they walked towards his car. Suddenly she felt his arm link with hers and Grace reached across with her other hand to secure it there. It was the first time they had shared such an intimate gesture, and Grace liked how it felt. As they walked down the main street, her arm entwined with her father's, she enjoyed their feeling of closeness. Was this what it would have felt like to have a father around when she was growing up?

'Patrick, can I ask you something?' she asked as they walked.

'Of course.'

She bit nervously on her lip. She had wanted to ask him this question for a few days now, but was never sure how to broach the topic. The last thing she wanted was to jeopardise their burgeoning relationship. They were still getting to know one another.

'I was wondering if you would mind me calling you... Dad.' She hoped she wasn't being premature; she knew she they couldn't make-up for all those years of absence overnight. She couldn't be angry with her mum or with Patrick for what had happened in the past; they had both been victims of Mrs Cavendish's and Tabitha's manipulation, but she was so grateful she was finally getting the chance to get to know her father.

He grinned back at her and squeezed her hand inside his own. 'Nothing in this world would make me happier.'

28

When Maggie came into the kitchen the next morning, Grace was already sitting at the kitchen table, wrapped in her mother's old dressing gown. For a moment it was like having Rosa sitting at the table again. Maggie's heart filled with pain at the likeness between Grace and her mother. Grace was hunched over her laptop as usual. Now that she had met the bank manager, Maggie had assumed she would be taking a break from her business plan for a while, but apparently not.

'Oh, good morning,' Grace said, closing the laptop when Maggie came into the room.

Maggie walked over and filled the kettle before putting it on the Aga. She needed a coffee – her head was fuzzy from the wine the night before.

'Well, how did it go?' she asked, joining Grace at the table. Grace had texted her the evening before to say the meeting had gone okay, but hadn't given any detail. She was in bed by the time Maggie got home, and Maggie was dying to hear how the meeting had gone.

'It was like an interrogation. They really put us through our paces.' Grace exhaled heavily. 'They were only short of asking me what I ate for breakfast on my first day of playschool!'

Maggie laughed. 'And what about Patrick? How was he in there?' Patrick seemed to live in his own world half the time, and Maggie hoped he'd made a good impression on the bank manager.

'We were a good team. I presented the facts and figures and my vision for Cavendish Hall, and he answered questions about the history of the house, the work that needs to be undertaken and all of that. It was good to have him there for support. I couldn't have done it without him.'

'I'm glad to hear that. So when will they let you know?'

'They said it'll be a couple of days, but it's only been a few hours and I'm already getting impatient. I'm not good at waiting. If we don't get this loan – well, I don't want to think about it...'

'You will,' Maggie encouraged.

'So, anyway, enough about the bank – how was your date?'

'It wasn't a date—' Maggie began.

'Whatever you want to call it.' Grace shook her head in exasperation. 'How did it go?'

'We had a lovely time. The restaurant was half-empty, though – poor Tadgh's business has been decimated.'

'That's awful. Has he managed to find any proof yet that the Steak House is behind it all?'

Maggie had filled Grace in on the latest twist in the story.

'Not yet, but hopefully he'll get to the bottom of it soon.'

The kettle whistled on the Aga. Maggie got up, made the

coffee then brought the pot and two mugs to the table before sitting down again. As she poured the coffee, she noticed Grace was looking oddly at her.

'What?' Maggie asked, trying her best to sound nonchalant.

'There's something you aren't telling me,' Grace probed.

'No, there isn't.' Maggie tried to keep her face neutral. She didn't want Grace to pick up on anything. The truth was, Maggie had been awake into the early hours thinking about what Liam had said to her. She had tossed and turned contemplating it all night long. She felt as though a curtain had been pulled back and she was seeing a new world full of possibility and second chances. He had spoken so directly, so honestly, and it had made her fizz from her toes right up along her body to the very tips of her fingers. But in the cold light of day, the warm, fuzzy feeling she had experienced as Liam had walked her home afterwards had evaporated. When she was alone in her cottage once more, she had come back down to reality like an old helium balloon. As she lay in bed that night, watching shadows flicker across the ceiling, doubts about Liam's intentions sprang into her mind. She knew he was a gentleman – that was never in question – but she wondered how well he knew himself. Even though it had been six years since Ingrid had passed away, Maggie knew that he still missed her. She wondered if he was ready to jump into something new. She could fall for him, only for him to realise that it was too soon – and where would that leave her? She couldn't risk opening her heart again, only to be hurt. She had spent a long time building herself back up, piece by piece, brick by brick, after Denis, and over time she had managed to regain her confidence and self-worth. She couldn't let it be destroyed by another man.

And their age was another thing that bothered her. If they did decide to try it out, how did one do romance these days? They were in their fifties. It had been so long since she had been intimate with someone – even the thought of kissing a man brought her out in a sweat. Would she remember what to do? Had things changed so drastically in all those years?

'Spit it out, Maggie. You're a terrible liar.' Grace ordered.

'Oh, all right.' Maggie sighed. She knew that Grace could see right through her. 'Liam said something to me...'

'What is it?'

'Well ... that he has feelings for me.'

'Oh, Maggie, that is amazing.' Grace beamed. 'I thought there was a spark between you both all right, but I didn't know if either of you could see it. I'm so happy for you.' She jumped up from her chair, came around the table and squeezed her aunt hard.

'Woah there, back up the horse, Gracie.' Maggie pulled back from Grace's embrace. 'I'm a bit long in the tooth for love.'

'Says who?' Grace asked, sitting back down.

'Ah, Grace, you're the one who should be telling me about boyfriends, not the other way around. Anyway, the last time I let a man into my life it ended up being a disaster.'

'That was a long time ago, Maggie.'

'I don't know.' Maggie sighed. 'It's different at my age. And Liam has been through a lot with losing Ingrid. I don't know if he's ready for romance. He might just be looking for a friend.'

'How will you ever know unless you open the door to your heart? Take a leap of faith. Give love a chance.'

Maggie fell silent as she pondered what Grace had said.

Was love really hers for the taking if she was just brave enough to let it in? Could she love again?

29

Penny felt as if the vibration of drills and hammers had been boring holes through her brain all morning. Some construction work had begun in the old drapery unit next door, and nobody seemed to know what was happening.

'I can't hear a word you're saying,' Ruairí cried, asking Penny to repeat what she had said for the third time.

'I said, what do you think they're doing?' she shouted again.

'Who knows?' Ruairí threw his hands up in frustration, then went to wipe down some tables that had been hastily vacated by customers who couldn't stand the noise.

'I didn't get any notice about works taking place,' he shouted back at her.

'Where on earth is that hullabaloo coming from?' Mrs Manning said, frowning, as she placed her teacup down on its saucer.

'There seems to be some work going on in the old drapery next door,' Ruairí shouted back to her.

'I don't know how you two can stand it. My head feels like it could explode.'

'I'm sorry, Mrs Manning – you're not the only one to complain,' he said, shaking his head in despair.

'I'm going to go,' she said, bending gingerly to retrieve her handbag from the floor then standing up. 'I can't stand another minute of it.' She steadied herself on her walking stick and slowly made her way towards the door. She was frail on her feet these days.

Penny rushed over to hold the door open for her. 'Hopefully they'll be finished by tomorrow,' Penny said apologetically.

A few minutes later Sarah arrived, wheeling a double pram. Having been born three months premature, her twins had only just reached their actual due date and Sarah and Greg were starting to feel a little braver about venturing outside with them now.

'How are you, Sarah, my dear, and those gorgeous twins?' Ruairí called, trying to be heard over the cacophony.

'Would you believe me if I said I was tired?' Although her eyes looked red and puffy, there was a glow in her smile that told them she was content. 'I badly need a coffee.'

'I'll put an extra shot in there.' Ruairí winked and began to grind the beans.

Penny peeped into the pram where Della-Alice and Emily, two pink-faced bundles, were sound asleep. 'They're beautiful,' she remarked.

'They're thriving – we're blessed to see them doing so well.' Sarah smiled lovingly at her daughters. 'What's going on next door?' she asked. 'They're making a lot of noise.'

Ruairí shrugged. 'It's been going on all morning. We don't know what they're doing.'

'On second thoughts, I'd better take my coffee to go, Ruairí. The babies will never sleep through that racket.'

After Ruairí had given Sarah her coffee, Penny held the door for Sarah. 'Maybe I should go in and see what's going on next door,' Penny suggested when she returned behind the counter.

'You could ask them to try and keep the noise down a little. We'll have no customers left at this rate,' Ruairí said, surveying the near-empty café.

'You hold the fort, I'll be right back,' Penny said. She stepped outside the café and bumped straight into Tadgh, who was standing on the pavement looking at the unit next door. 'What's wrong?' she asked, following his line of sight to where a white van with the Steak House logo emblazoned across the side was parked on the footpath. They watched as construction workers unloaded materials from the back of the van and carried them into the unit.

'So that's what's going on,' Penny said as it all clicked into place. 'They've been making so much noise all morning!'

'I feel like going in there and giving them a piece of my mind,' Tadgh said.

'Well why don't you?' Penny asked.

'But what would I say? We don't know for sure that it's them causing all the trouble.'

Penny cocked her head sceptically. 'We all know it's them.' She linked his arm. 'Come on, let's go and find out what's going on.'

The door was open, so they went inside to find a hive of workers busy fitting out the interior.

'Sorry there–' A worker carrying long planks of wood beneath his arm called and they stepped to one side to let him through.

'Is the foreman around?' Tadgh asked the man as he passed.

'Declan?' the man called over to another man who was studying some plans across the room. He turned around and made his way over to them. He was wearing a hard hat and high-vis jacket but had a suit underneath. He signalled for his workmen to stop making noise. 'Declan Kenny is the name,' he greeted Penny and Tadgh. 'What can I do for you?'

'I'm Penny Murphy,' Penny began. 'I work in the café next door, and we're getting a lot of complaints from our customers about the noise.'

'Well, we have to do the works.' Declan shrugged. 'We've got a tight schedule to stick to so the good people of Inishbeg Cove can have their own branch of Steak House.' He smiled, but the corners of his lips never moved.

'So this is where you're opening?' Tadgh asked.

'Yes. Inishbeg Cove will be our fifty-fourth branch,' he said proudly. 'And might I ask who you are?'

'Tadgh O'Reilly. I own the restaurant up on the cliff.'

Declan's eyes sparked with recognition. 'Ah, the famous Tadgh – to what do I owe the pleasure?' He held out his hand. 'Nice to finally meet the competition.'

'There's plenty room for us both,' Tadgh said.

'Oh, I don't know about that. I guess time will tell.' He smirked, and Penny bristled with anger. She couldn't let it go. She had to ask.

'Are you the person who has been trying to shut down Tadgh's business over the last few weeks?' she asked.

'Now, now, a good businessman never reveals his secrets.' Declan shook his head.

'Well, taking down a small restaurant to ensure your

own success isn't fair,' Penny continued, feeling bolder, sure she was on the right track.

'That's business.' Declan shrugged.

'It's underhand,' Tadgh said. 'It might be how *you* do business, but it's not how *I* do things.'

'There's a reason why we're Ireland's most successful chain of restaurants. We'll see whose strategy is better in a few weeks. We'll wipe the floor with you,' Declan sneered.

'But why are you even opening here? There are so many other places you could have opened with far bigger populations than Inishbeg Cove,' Tadgh said.

'You've created a nice catchment of foodies here, Tadgh. Inishbeg Cove might only be a dot on the map, but it has a reputation for good food. People travel from miles around to eat here. Plus...' Declan tapped the side of his nose. 'The first rule of business is to follow the market.'

'Even so, you could have opened and let customers decide where they want to eat. If that means Steak House is the winner, then so be it, but destroying my reputation so your restaurant can get a head start is nasty!'

'Come on, Tadgh, you know how these things work. You've been sitting on a little gold mine here. Don't be greedy. You've had this place all to yourself for long enough, and now it's time to share.' Declan spoke in the tone a parent might use for a toddler who wouldn't share their toys.

'But making false accusations and writing fake reviews isn't fair! For weeks now I've been doubting my ability to run my restaurant. I thought I'd lost my touch, but you've been out to shut me down all along!' Tadgh couldn't keep emotion from creeping into his voice.

'Can't handle a little competition, Tadgh?' Declan needled him.

'Competition?' Tadgh cried. 'You published a false review, lied about getting food poisoning and manufactured a landslide! How am I meant to compete with that?'

Declan sniggered. 'You can't prove I did all that.'

'But I can,' Penny announced, producing her phone from her coat pocket. 'I've recorded the whole conversation.'

'Th-that's illegal!' Declan shouted, his faux charm instantly evaporating. 'You can't record without permission.' He stepped forward to snatch her phone from her but Tadgh moved between them, blocking him. The workmen, who hadn't been paying them any attention, were suddenly watching the scene, agog.

'I wonder how many other restaurants you've closed down in the same way?' Tadgh asked. 'I think it's time that people knew about your dirty tactics and how you've managed to expand your chain so quickly.'

'Ah, come on, Tadgh, I think you've misunderstood me…' Declan tried to explain.

'Oh, I think we're very clear on what's gone on here,' Tadgh retorted. 'The newspapers would be interested in this little story, don't you think?'

By now the workmen had all downed tools, transfixed by the drama unfolding before their eyes.

'What the hell are you looking at?' Declan Kenny roared, his eyes ablaze as he looked at them. 'Get back to work!'

'A story like this could take down your whole chain,' Tadgh continued, unperturbed, knowing Declan Kenny was rattled now.

'If you don't pack up your stuff and get the hell out of Inishbeg Cove, I'm going to report you to An Garda Síochána,' Penny threatened.

'And I'm sure the county council might have something

to say about how you've wasted their time by making fake complaints...' Tadgh added.

Declan hesitated, his gaze darting around, before eventually opening his mouth to speak. 'Do you know what? I was never really sure about Inishbeg Cove. When I was here during the summer, it was booming, but look at it now – it's like a ghost town! It's in the middle of nowhere – it takes half a day to get here. You've made up my mind for me.' He looked at Tadgh and Penny. 'This backwater place isn't worth my time,' he spat. 'I'm pulling the plug here. You're welcome to it, Tadgh!'

30

Grace was already up when a bleary-eyed Maggie came into the kitchen on Monday morning. She felt as though she hadn't slept a wink the night before – actually, it felt as though she hadn't slept properly since her dinner with Liam on Friday. All kinds of things had been spinning around in her head. The more she thought about it, the more she was sure it had been the alcohol talking. What on earth would a kind, handsome man like Liam see in her? She had spent the weekend trying to press down her feelings again, squash them back inside, but it was like trying to wrestle a jack-in-the-box back into its box. No matter how often she told herself not to, her stomach flipped every time she thought about Liam.

'Are you not coming for a swim this morning?' Maggie asked Grace with a yawn. She shuffled into the kitchen in her slippers and filled the kettle before putting it on the stove. As usual, Grace was sitting at the table working on her laptop. She wasn't wrapped in her fleecy dressing gown, however; instead, she wore a pretty tea dress with suede boots – definitely not the sort of clothing to be heading down to the chilly cove in.

Grace shook her head. 'Sorry, I can't today. I need to go through some more of the legal paperwork with Patrick.'

'Hopefully you might hear from the bank this week,' Maggie said. She knew it was weighing heavily on Grace's mind.

'They said it would take a couple of days but who knows.' She sighed as her face creased in worry. 'What if they turn us down?'

'Try to stay positive, Gracie. Patrick said you were amazing in there. He said you had answers for every curve ball they threw your way and you were unflappable.'

Grace had invited Patrick over to the cottage for lunch the day before and Maggie had been surprised to find she had actually enjoyed the afternoon. She had nearly choked on a piece of chicken when Grace had called Patrick 'Dad' though, but Patrick didn't bat an eyelid and Maggie realised that it obviously wasn't the first time Grace had referred to him like that. In fact, he had seemed delighted by it. She noticed that his face shone whenever Grace was around. It was impossible not to notice how his eyes lit with adoration every time he looked at his daughter, and Maggie knew he was grateful to finally have the chance to get to know her. She couldn't help wondering what kind of a relationship they would have had if Rosa had allowed him to be a part of Grace's life growing up. There was no doubting his feelings for his daughter. Maggie knew that the time had come to put past hurts behind them, and she dearly hoped that Grace and Patrick could make up for all the missing years.

'I think he was just being kind. I was a nervous wreck.' Grace began to wind up her laptop charger and placed it in her bag. She picked up her folder of paperwork and put it in too. 'I'd better go,' she said, giving Maggie a kiss on the cheek. On her way out she lifted a slice of toast out of the toaster, put it between her teeth, slid her arms into her coat sleeves then headed out the door.

After Grace had gone, Maggie gathered her towel and flask and stepped out into the damp, drizzly day, pulling the cottage door closed behind her. She hadn't seen Liam since their dinner on Friday evening and she was both looking forward to and dreading the swim that morning. As she walked down to the cove, butterflies began to career around inside her stomach. She just hoped there wouldn't be any lingering awkwardness; she wanted to forget what Liam had said and get on with things.

She made her way through the dunes and saw that Liam was already there, standing beside the rocks chatting to the rest of the group. Her heart picked up at the sight of him, and the butterflies multiplied inside her. *Stop it, Maggie,* she warned herself. *Just pretend nothing happened.*

'Hi Liam,' she began as she reached them.

'How are you, Maggie?' He wouldn't meet her eyes. Maggie could tell he was finding this just as awkward as she was. Without saying anything else, they undressed and made their way into the water, where all thoughts of embarrassment and awkwardness were soon forgotten as the cold water hit them. Maggie lay back, letting waves bob her, looking up at the dull sky, which was thick with cloud.

After they had finished, they dried off, had a hot drink and passed around the biscuits. The group chatted about the weather and their plans for the week. Maggie was relieved that when they were in the group, it seemed to be business as usual for them. Perhaps they might be able to put their initial awkwardness behind them, she hoped.

After everyone had dressed, they said their goodbyes and began to head their separate ways.

'Can I walk with you?' Liam asked Maggie as she waved off the others.

'Of course,' Maggie replied. They had walked home together many times before, but now he obviously felt the need to ask permission. Maggie hated that everything had changed between them.

As they walked along the headland, their conversation was stilted. The green fields spread out like a velvet carpet on one side of the road, and on the other side the land sloped down towards the sea. A blanket of mist had begun to fall, and droplets hung like diamonds from the hedgerows. They stood in close to the ditch as a car went past, then they waved at the driver and walked on. The water glistened like polished steel below them. Maggie was racking her brain trying to think of something to say, but the harder her mind worked, the more her brain seemed to freeze. She was never normally stuck for words, but they had deserted her that morning. And it seemed as though Liam wasn't faring much better. Usually they laughed and joked together, but this was painfully awkward.

'Would you like to come in for a cuppa?' Maggie said when they reached her cottage, because that was all she could think of to say.

'That would be lovely.'

Her heart sank. She had expected him to make an excuse and go home, but now they were going to have to prolong the embarrassment.

Maggie opened the door and Liam stepped inside after her and removed his gloves, followed by his coat. Maggie filled the kettle and, when it whistled on the stove, she made the tea. She set the pot down on the table and took a seat opposite Liam.

'I hope I didn't scare you off the other day,' Liam began.

Oh no, Maggie groaned internally. So they were going to have this conversation after all. He was going to dive straight in and not even wait until she had taken a sip from her mug.

'Of course not,' she said, clasping the mug, glad to have something to do with her hands.

Silence fell between them until Liam spoke again. 'I meant what I said,' he went on. 'I'll be fifty-five on Friday. I like to think I've lived long enough to know that when you find someone special, you hold on to them with both hands.' His dark eyes locked with hers, forcing her to look at him. 'When you get to our age, there's no point beating around the bush.'

Maggie felt her heart start to ratchet and her stomach began to spin. 'I don't know, Liam.' She sighed and put her mug down on the table. 'Aren't we too old?'

'Are we? I don't remember ever hearing that there was an age limit on romance.'

'Ah, I had given up on all of that stuff. I thought it was a young person's game, and then you came along and knocked me off my feet so I don't know which end of me is up any more. I just feel so unsure.'

'And what does your heart say?'

'To take a chance.'

'Well, there's your answer. Ever since I met you that day down in the cove, I can't help thinking how it was fate. Whenever you're around, well… I feel that the sun shines a little brighter, the bird song sounds a little sharper, and everything is better in the world. and whenever you leave, it's like somebody twisted a dimmer switch on my day and everything mutes down again. I haven't felt this way in years and it's both exhilarating and a little terrifying, if I'm honest.'

'It's been a long time all right,' Maggie agreed.

'It's been a long time for both of us, but I can finally see that there is still life out there to be lived, fun to be had...' He paused. 'Maybe even love to take a chance on, if you'll have me?' He reached for her hand across the table, before pulling her upright so that they were standing. Liam moved closer to Maggie, so close that his stubble brushed her cheek. Her skin started to tingle and lightning bolts began shooting around her body. He was standing so close to her. No man had stood this close to her in years. Especially one this attractive. Their faces were just inches apart, and she could see into the depths of his kindly brown eyes. She knew he was a good, honest man. All the things that Maggie thought wrong with her – her loud, extroverted nature, her clumsiness – turned out to be the things that Liam liked best. It was hard to fathom that he liked her just as she was. He had seen her at her worst, her dimpled thighs and her wobbly bits jiggling as she ran into the cold water, and he *still* liked her.

He reached up and cupped her face and her skin came alive at his touch. He pulled her closer still and she held her breath as his lips, warm and full, finally met hers. His mouth searched hers. She was surprised to discover that it was like putting her feet on the pedals of a bike: it all came back to her and her body responded as it remembered what to do. All her doubts and worries faded away. At that moment it was just her and Liam, two people who had finally found what they had been searching for at last.

31

A few days later Maggie picked her way through the silvery marram grass, climbing up the dunes after her swim. The charcoal sky was heavy above and rain clouds were pushing in off the Atlantic. Liam hadn't joined her that morning because he had had to travel to Dublin for a Christmas lunch with his editor. Although she knew she would see him later – she was cooking dinner for him that night – she missed his company. She was telling herself to take things slowly, but her heart didn't seem to be getting the message. Just a few weeks ago she had never set eyes on the man, but her swim that morning had felt a little lacklustre, just because he wasn't there. As she had bathed in the bosom of the water, her body weightless in the swell as it surged towards the shore, she realised how much the ocean had given her. It wasn't just the calm it brought to her mind; the sea had healed her wounded heart after Denis had fractured it all those years ago. When she had been numbed by grief after Rosa's death, the cold water was the only thing that could cut through the shock and made her feel that she was still alive. The sea – where life was created but could be stolen just as fast – had almost turned on her too, but instead it had brought Liam into her life when she had given up hope of ever finding love again.

As she reached the café, she saw the Steak House van being loaded with catering equipment. She stood and watched for a moment, savouring the scene. She had been wide-eyed with disbelief when Tadgh and Penny had recounted to her what had happened when they confronted Declan Kenny. Tadgh had proudly recalled, his arm slung around Penny's waist, how Penny's threat to inform the Gardaí had sent Declan running. Maggie was glad that the odious man had finally got his comeuppance. Tadgh had decided that it was enough that Steak House was pulling out of Inishbeg Cove; he wouldn't report Declan Kenny to the guards, but he was clearly a more forgiving person than she was. Maggie would have taken him to the cleaners if it had been up to her.

She pushed open the café door, glad to exchange the squally day outside for the warmth of the café. Ruairí had put up a real Christmas tree and the intoxicating scent of pine and coffee filled the air.

'Well, it looks like Steak House has finally gone away with its tail between its legs,' Maggie announced. 'I saw a van outside, loading up the last of the catering equipment.'

'Yes, they've been packing up all morning. Good riddance to them! If they had played fairly, it could all have been different. There could have been room for both restaurants,' Ruairí said.

'Tadgh must be relieved,' Maggie said.

'He is, and his bookings have really picked up over the last few days,' Penny added. 'He's so happy to be back doing what he loves.'

'Isn't that marvellous news?' Maggie clapped her hands.

'I knew once the villagers realised what was happening, they'd all be out in force behind him.'

'Any word on Grace's loan yet?' Ruairí asked. They knew Grace was anxiously waiting for news. It had almost been a week since she had met the bank manager; she and Patrick had hoped they would have heard something by now.

'No word yet.' Maggie sighed. 'The poor thing is beside herself with worry. She phoned the bank yesterday for an update, only to be told that the manager in Ballymcconnell had referred it higher up the chain to his area manager, so she has a while yet to wait. I didn't say it to Grace, but it doesn't sound good if the local manager felt it was too risky a decision for him to make on his own, does it? I just hope she gets word before Christmas, or the waiting will drive her demented.'

'Oh dear, well, we can't lose hope yet. I'll keep everything crossed for her,' Ruairí said.

'Thanks, Ruairí. She could use a bit of good news after the last few months. Look, the reason I came in is that it's Liam's birthday tomorrow. He doesn't know I'm doing this, so say nothing if you see him, but I was hoping to surprise him by taking him for a few drinks in The Anchor.' Maggie knew Liam wasn't one for being the centre of attention, so she hoped he wouldn't mind her organising it. He had insisted to Maggie that he didn't want any fuss, but he had become special to her over the last few weeks and she wanted to make an effort for his birthday. 'The sea-swimmers are going to come along too.'

Ruairí raised his brows. 'You and Liam seem to be very pally these days,' he teased.

Maggie blushed. She was still trying to get used to it. She felt like a giddy teenager whenever Liam was around. He had held her hand as they had entered the café after their swim yesterday, and tiny bubbles had fizzed in her tummy. She'd forgotten the excitement of a new relationship – when you wanted to be around the person all the time and how you counted down the minutes until you were with them again. 'It's early days for us, but so far so good,' she admitted.

'I'm happy for you,' Ruairí said. 'Maybe there's hope for me yet.'

'Of course there is. If romance can come knocking on my door, there's hope for anyone.' She laughed. 'So will you come?'

'I wouldn't miss it.'

Maggie turned to Penny. 'What about you, Penny? And Tadgh?'

'Tadgh has a full house tomorrow night for the first time in weeks, so he definitely won't be able to come, but I'm sure my parents will be only too glad of the chance to mind Lucy for the night,' Penny said, 'so count me in. Who knows? Tadgh might be able to join us after service.'

'Great stuff.' Maggie beamed, excited to see her plans coming together. 'We'll have to raise a toast to Tadgh being back in business again. Will we say around eight?'

'We'll see you then.'

'And remember, say nothing if you see Liam!' she warned with a wink as she left the café.

32

The next day Maggie removed the cake from the box that Ruairí had put it in when she had bought it earlier in the café and balanced it on the palm of her hand, while she used her other hand to take out the candle she had bought in O'Herlihy's and push it deep into the rich chocolate ganache. Then she rapped the knocker of Sea Spray cottage and waited. Liam appeared after a moment, barefoot and dressed in jeans and a T-shirt.

'Maggie,' he began, clearly surprised when he saw the cake. 'You remembered!' He ran a hand through his tousled hair, and Maggie felt her heart somersault at the sight of him. He was so attractive, she still had to pinch herself to believe that they were together.

'Happy birthday to you,' she sang. 'Happy birthday to you, happy birthday dear Liaaaam – oh, I think I'll spare you the rest.' She trailed off when the song climbed higher.

'Come on in.' He laughed.

She went inside and Liam closed the door behind her. She found a plate in the press and set the cake down onto it.

Then she rooted around in her bag for the gift she had brought.

'You shouldn't have,' he said, taking it from her and tearing open the paper.

'It's only something small.'

'A flask.' He unwrapped the present and turned it around in his hands. 'And it even has my name engraved on it.'

'Now that you're a fully-fledged Inishbeg Cove sea-swimmer, I thought it was high time you had your own flask.'

They had recently had the conversation about Liam's plans and he had tentatively asked her what she would think about him staying in the village for the foreseeable future. He had seemed almost nervous as he broached the subject, perhaps worrying that it would be too much, too soon, for her, but Maggie had thrown her arms around his neck and planted a kiss on his lips in joy. As they had begun to spend more and more time together, a feeling of trepidation about his return to Dublin had been hanging over her. She had been nervous about having a long-distance relationship, and so she had been overjoyed when he told her that he would be happy to stay on in Inishbeg Cove if she was okay with it. His sons had both flown the nest and being a writer meant he could work anywhere, so he wasn't tied down. She was excited that he was giving their relationship every chance; it seemed that he wanted it to work just as much as she did.

'Thank you, Maggie.' Liam smiled. 'I'll have no excuse not to bring my own coffee now.'

'Well, you can't keep sponging off me all the time,' she teased.

'This is turning into a lovely birthday. Normally the day

tends to slip past without any fuss. Why don't I cook something for us tonight?' he offered.

She thought about the surprise party she had organised for him at The Anchor and felt her stomach lurch. For all she knew, he might hate it; some people loathed surprises, but she had everything arranged and it was too late to back out now. She just needed to get him to the pub without arousing his suspicions. 'We can't have you cooking on your birthday! How about we go to The Anchor for a meal?' she suggested.

'All right then,' Liam agreed. 'That sounds like a plan.'

'Now, have you any matches so I can light this candle?' Maggie asked.

'It's been a long time since I've blown out candles on my birthday cake,' Liam said, rummaging in a kitchen drawer.

'Nonsense.' Maggie tutted. 'You're never too old for candles on your cake.'

Liam eventually found some matches. She was just about to open the box when there was a knock at the door.

'Who could that be?' Liam asked. He was about to get up and answer it when the door was pushed open and two broad-shouldered young men barrelled through, giving Maggie an awful fright.

'Happy birthday!' they announced, big grins on their faces. 'Oh...' Their faces fell when they spotted Maggie sitting at the table. 'You've got company.'

'What are you two doing here?' a shocked Liam asked, jumping up and embracing the young men. 'I thought you weren't coming until Christmas Eve!'

'We wanted to surprise you for your birthday,' the older of the two explained.

Liam turned to Maggie. 'Maggie, I'd like you to meet

Ultan.' Liam pointed to the older man. 'And Lorcan.' He stood proudly between both boys. 'These are my sons.'

His sons. Oh God. They were both tall and dark-featured and now Maggie could see their resemblance to Liam. Her palms were clammy. She felt as though they had been caught doing something wrong, even though they were only sitting at the table together. She was keenly aware that it was early days in their relationship – it was far too early to be meeting his adult children. She had thought it would be a few months before they reached this stage – that was, if they even got that far.

Liam had told her that the boys would be spending Christmas in Inishbeg Cove with him, but she had planned on giving him space to spend time with his sons for a few days. Now that they were standing here, she was unsure what to say or what way to act. This was new ground for her; she had never dated a widower before, let alone one with adult children, and she wasn't sure of the protocol. Would Liam want her to pretend they were just friends? But Ultan and Lorcan weren't children; they would see right through any attempts to pull the wool over their eyes. Obviously she knew that if she and Liam were serious, she would need to meet his sons, but now felt too soon. What if they were still upset by the loss of their mother? They might not be ready to see their father move on with another woman. Just when things were starting to go well between them... She should have known that something would happen to put a spanner in the works.

Before she could ruminate any longer, she felt a pair of arms being thrown around her and she was squeezed tightly.

'I'm so glad to finally meet the famous Maggie!' Ultan gushed.

Then Lorcan stepped forward to shake her hand. 'Dad hasn't stopped talking about you.' He grinned as he pumped her hand.

Maggie felt as though she was sitting on a spinning top, she was dizzy trying to keep up with them. 'I-I see...' was all she managed to stammer. She risked a glance at Liam, and saw heat creeping up along his face.

'Boys, you're making a show of me!' Liam chided. 'Oh, who am I kidding? It's all true.' He laughed.

Maggie felt a rush of pleasure – Liam had already told his sons about her! She slowly started to relax. Judging by their warm reaction and friendliness, she saw no reservations about their father embarking on a new relationship. She exhaled heavily and her shoulders climbed down from her ears.

'It's lovely to meet you both.' Maggie smiled at them. 'You timed it well, lads – you're just in time for cake.'

~

THAT NIGHT MAGGIE and Grace walked into The Anchor and breathed in the beery smell infused with the peat of the fire. Skipper, the elderly sheepdog, grey around the muzzle, was sprawled in front of the hearth and a Christmas tree with white fairy lights twinkled in the corner. Skipper opened his eyes and gave a thump of his tail before falling back asleep again. The pub was warm and inviting, with a low buzz of chatter which was only broken by peals of laughter every now and again. Since it was a Friday night in the run-up to Christmas, the bar was busy and all the seats were already taken. Some people were eating at tables and a few of the older village men, wearing flat caps, sat on stools at the bar while Jim, the barman, wiped down the counter.

A few of the swimmers were already gathered around a table down at the end of the pub. Maggie spotted Imelda, Laura and Frank, and Ruairí and Penny were with them. They headed over and greeted everyone.

'Hello, everyone!' Maggie cried. 'I told Liam I'd meet him at quarter past, so he should be here soon. I can't tell you how many times I nearly let it slip today. I just hope he won't mind me surprising him like this,' she said anxiously.

'Try not to worry,' Grace assured her. 'We don't have to make a big deal of it – it's just a few friends gathered to wish him a happy birthday.'

'You're right,' Maggie said, but it didn't stop the nerves careering around inside her tummy. Just then she spotted Liam, Ultan and Lorcan making their way across the pub towards them.

'Oh, look, he's coming!' she told the others.

'Surprise!' They cheered when Liam reached them.

'What are you all doing here?' he asked, looking around at them all in amazement. He turned to Maggie in shock. 'I thought I was just meeting you and Grace?'

'We wanted to surprise you,' Maggie explained.

'Well thank you, Maggie.' Liam beamed at her as he looked around at the gathering before pulling her into a hug. 'What a lovely idea. Everyone, these are my sons, Ultan and Lorcan.'

'Happy birthday, Liam.' Penny stepped forward and hugged him. 'This is from me and Tadgh. He hopes to join us later.' She handed him a bottle of Jameson whiskey. 'I don't know what your usual tipple is, but I figure you can't go wrong with whiskey.'

'You really shouldn't have, but thank you,' Liam said, taking the bag from her, looking a little overwhelmed by the fuss the gang were making of him.

'So what age are you then, birthday boy?' Ruairí asked.

'Fifty-five. Would you believe, the boys gave me a pair of slippers? I know I'm getting on, but I'm not ready for a pipe and slippers just yet.' Liam laughed.

'You're lucky it wasn't a voucher for dentures.' Lorcan elbowed him playfully.

Liam shook his head in faux exasperation. 'Do you see what I have to put up with?'

'Never mind them. You're fifty-five and fabulous,' Maggie said, giving his arm a squeeze.

'I'll get a round in. What will you all have?' Liam asked.

'But it's your birthday!' Maggie protested.

'I insist – it's my way to say thanks to everyone for coming here tonight and for welcoming me so wholeheartedly to the village.'

'Okay then, but the next one is on me,' Maggie said.

'Welcome to the world of modern dating, Dad,' Ultan quipped, clapping his father on the back. 'It's all split bills and shared rounds these days.'

Liam laughed and, after he had taken everyone's order, he made his way up to Jim at the bar. A few minutes later Liam, assisted by Lorcan, returned with the drinks and handed them out. The banter between Ultan and Lorcan was good craic, and they had everyone in stitches. Liam hadn't stopped smiling since he had arrived. As Maggie looked around at the little group, she could tell that everyone was enjoying the evening. She was glad she had made the effort to bring them all together.

After a while Maggie felt a rush of cold air and saw the door open. She looked over to see who was arriving, and was surprised to see Patrick. Perhaps Grace had invited him, she thought, but Maggie quickly realised, from the urgency on his face as he hurried across the bar towards them, that it wasn't just a social visit. She hoped nothing was wrong.

'Is everything okay?' she asked when he neared her.

'Is Grace here?' he said quickly, looking around. 'I've been trying to call her—'

'Over there.' Maggie pointed to where Grace was chatting with Ultan. She threw her head back, giggling at something he had said. Although they had only just met, Maggie had noticed that the two of them really seemed to have hit off. 'Grace?' Maggie called over to her, but she didn't hear her over the din. 'Grace!' she called again, louder this time.

Grace turned around. When she saw her father, she came over. 'Is everything okay, Dad?'

'I've been trying to call you—'

'Sorry, my phone is in my handbag. I haven't checked it in a while. What is it?'

'The bank left a voice message for me earlier, but I was out with Donie on the farm. I've only just listened to it. They said they couldn't reach you.'

Grace went pale. 'And?'

'We got the loan!' he announced, a grin spreading across his face.

Grace let out a squeal of excitement and Patrick lifted her up and swung her around in a circle.

'Oh, that's fantastic!' Maggie cried. As soon as Patrick had put Grace back on the ground, Maggie threw her arms around her niece. 'You deserve this, Gracie. I'm proud of you.'

'I was starting to doubt it was going to happen,' Grace said, tears of happiness filling her eyes. As the days had passed, hope of a positive outcome had begun to fade for Grace.

'They told me they'll send a formal loan offer by close of business on Monday!' Patrick went on.

'Oh, thank you, Patrick.' Grace began to sob as the news began to sink in. She could start making plans now: she could finally start making her dream a reality.

'This calls for a celebration!' Maggie turned towards the bar and called up to Jim. 'Can we get a bottle of something bubbly, please?'

Maggie shook Patrick's hand. 'And congratulations to you too. I'm really happy for you both.'

'Well, now all the fun begins.' Patrick smiled.

After a few minutes Jim presented them with a champagne bottle and a tray of flutes for everyone. Grace popped the cork and golden nectar spilled over the rim of the bottle.

'To Cavendish Hall!' they toasted once everyone had a glass in their hand.

'And Grace!' Patrick chimed in.

'And Grace,' they repeated.

Liam moved closer to Maggie and draped an arm around her shoulder as they watched the celebrations. She liked the weight of it there. It made her feel secure, as if he was hers and she was his. As Maggie looked around the pub at their little gathering, she felt herself get caught up in a wave of emotion for them – all these people who had come to mean so much to her. Grace's face was animated with joy as she chatted with her father. Despite her initial reservations about Patrick, Maggie was glad that he and Grace had finally got to know one another. Their new adventure of restoring Cavendish Hall meant her niece would be staying in the village for the foreseeable future but, more importantly, it had given Grace a new passion in life.

And then there was Liam. A good, decent man who made her feel like the most important woman in the world.

She still had to pinch herself that it was really her he had fallen for. They were at the beginning of something new and terrifying, but a feeling deep inside, told her to trust him, to open her heart and let him in.

The waters of Inishbeg Cove had brought all these people together, but they had done more than that: they had cradled them and bathed away their sorrows until they had each found happiness at last.

BOOKS BY IZZY BAYLISS

The Lily McDermott Series
The Girl I was Before
Baked with Love

~

The Inishbeg Cove Series
The Secrets of Inishbeg Cove
Coming Home to Inishbeg Cove
Escape to Inishbeg Cove

A LETTER FROM IZZY

Thank you so very much for reading *Escape to Inishbeg Cove*. I am touched that so many people have taken the Inishbeg Cove series to their hearts. I enjoy writing these stories so much and, after three books, I genuinely feel as if the village and its characters are real.

If you would like to keep up to date with my latest releases, please sign up to my newsletter on www.izzybayliss.com. I promise never to spam you, and you can unsubscribe at any time.

If you enjoyed *Escape to Inishbeg Cove*, I would really appreciate it if you could leave a short review on Amazon. Reviews help to get a book noticed by Amazon, which will then promote the book to new readers, so they are hugely important to us authors. It doesn't have to be long – just one line will do – and I will be forever grateful.

Thank you for reading.

Love, Izzy x

ACKNOWLEDGMENTS

To my gorgeous family, my husband Simon and our four children, Lila, Tom, Bea and Charlie, who are my world. Our trips to the west of Ireland have provided lots of inspiration for the Inishbeg Cove series but, more importantly, they have given me so many treasured memories.

I must also thank my dear friend and fellow author Janelle Brooke Harris for always being there with a listening ear – and for keeping me sane.

To Richie in More Visual, who has designed another great cover and is so easy to work with and to Jane Hammett for her brilliant edit; your eagle eye has definitely enriched this book.

I also owe a huge 'thank you' to the amazing blogging community, who have been so supportive of my books. I am always amazed at your enthusiasm and am grateful for all you do to help us authors spread the word about our books.

Last, thank you to you, my readers. Thank you for choosing my book from all the books out there! I hope you enjoyed it.

Izzy xx

ABOUT THE AUTHOR

Izzy Bayliss lives in Ireland with her husband and four young children and their hyperactive puggle. A romantic at heart, she loves nothing more than cosying up in front of a roaring fire with a good book. *Escape to Inishbeg Cove* is the third book Izzy has written in the hugely popular Inishbeg Cove series.

You can find out more about Izzy Bayliss at www.izzybayliss.com.

Izzy can also be found hanging about on Facebook @izzybaylissauthor and Twitter @izzybayliss.

She also writes emotional women's fiction as Caroline Finnerty.

Printed in Great Britain
by Amazon